Whispers in the Fog

It was nearly noon by the time Nancy and Bess left for their drive down the California coast. Twice Nancy pulled off onto a scenic overlook so Bess could snap a photo of the majestic hills and sea.

"All I know is—" Bess started to say. She interrupted herself when she glanced at Nancy. "What do you see?"

Nancy stared into the rearview mirror.

"Come on, tell me. What are you looking at? Who is it?" Bess repeated.

"I'm not sure," Nancy answered. "But when I slow down, he slows down. When I drive faster, he speeds up, too."

Nancy glanced at the car in her mirror. "He's coming faster," she said as she pressed down on the accelerator a little harder.

She looked up again. The car was charging toward her, filling her rearview mirror.

Nancy Drew
Mystery Stories

Available from MINSTREL Books

NANCY DREW® 153

WHISPERS IN THE FOG

CAROLYN KEENE

A MINSTREL® BOOK

Published by POCKET BOOKS
New York   London   Toronto   Sydney   Singapore

A MINSTREL PAPERBACK *Original*

A Minstrel Book published by
POCKET BOOKS, a division of Simon & Schuster Inc.
1230 Avenue of the Americas, New York, NY 10020

Copyright © 2000 by Simon & Schuster Inc.

ISBN: 0-671-04133-9

First Minstrel Books printing March 2000

10 9 8 7 6 5 4 3 2 1

NANCY DREW, A MINSTREL BOOK and colophon are registered trademarks of Simon & Schuster Inc.

Cover art by Ernie Norcia

Printed in the U.S.A.

Contents

WHISPERS IN THE FOG

1

A Surprise Visitor

The California sun felt warm on Nancy Drew's slender back. She stood beside the car she had picked up at the San Francisco airport and watched her friend George Fayne run up the steps of the small wood-frame house. The house, the sky, and Nancy's eyes were all the same shade of blue.

It had been a long flight and a long drive, and Nancy was happy to be out of the car at last.

"You made it!" said a tall girl, running out of the house and grabbing George in a big hug.

"Perfect instructions as always," George replied with a grin. "Hey, guys, this is Katie Firestone. Katie, these are my best friends from home—Nancy Drew, my cousin Bess Marvin, and Ned Nickerson."

Katie ushered them into her house and showed George her room.

"I wish I could put you all up," she said generously. "But it would get pretty cramped." An attractive twenty-year-old with brown hair, she had an athlete's body—tall, lithe, and strong.

Nancy and her friends had come from River Heights to a spot on the northern California coast near the tiny town of Seabreak. George had met Katie at a world sea kayaking competition and persuaded Nancy, Bess, and Ned to come to Seabreak for a vacation. To earn money Katie piloted her own whale-watching tourist boat, and January was a perfect month to watch the migrating whales.

They were all looking forward to seeing the whales and to training with Katie for sea kayaking.

"I love your house," Bess said. "It's so cute." Although Bess Marvin was George's cousin, they looked nothing alike. Bess had pale blue eyes and straw blond hair, without the reddish tones of Nancy's. George was slim and athletic, with dark hair and eyes. Bess's figure was fuller.

"Well, look quick," Katie said, with a toss of her long straight dark hair. "I've been working on it for two days in honor of your visit. I'm not the best housekeeper in the world, and things get out of hand quickly."

"Looks fine to me," Ned chimed in. "So, when do we start the kayak training? I'm ready." Ned was also tall, with clean-cut good looks. As captain of his school's football team, he was a natural athlete. He had been white-water kayaking and had come on the trip to get some experience kayaking in the surf.

"It's really too late for a workout now," Katie said. "But I've packed a picnic. I thought we'd bike around the area so I could show you some of my favorite places. It's really beautiful here."

"We'll need to go into town to rent bikes," George said.

"No, you won't," Katie said. "I've got seven or eight in the garage. Biking's a big hobby of mine— and it's great exercise to keep me in shape. I pick them up at yard sales and flea markets for nothing, rehaul them, and fix them up till they're good as new. Go on out and take your pick. Ned, I've even got a couple of men's bikes I keep for friends."

It took just a few minutes to pick bikes. From the back fender of Katie's red bike hung a sign with the name Firestone Whale Watching and Katie's phone number written on it.

Nancy followed Katie as they rode single file along the winding two-lane highway. To the left were fields of golden grasses leading to the Pacific Ocean, which was shining a bright blue in the late afternoon sun. To the right, more fields of green and gold ended at the foot of enormous hills covered with dark forests of redwoods and firs.

After a few more miles, Katie led them down a

narrow path toward the rugged coastal bluff. They parked their bikes and leaned them against a couple of cypress trees.

"Now, there's a sign you don't see in River Heights," Ned said.

Nancy followed his gaze to the short post topped with a rustic flat wood board. " 'Please don't shout,' " Nancy read aloud. " 'Sea lions use this beach as a nursery. Loud noises might disturb the mothers and their pups.' " She looked down at the foot of the bluff. Beyond the sandy shore were large outcroppings of rock that formed a network of small islands and jetties in the water. Sunbathing on the rocks, just a few yards from the shore, were a dozen sea lions, some with babies snuggled next to them.

"Let's go on down to the beach," Katie said. "Everybody grab something. Just leave the bikes up here—they'll be okay."

Bess and George grabbed their backpacks and followed Katie down the wooden-plank steps secured into the rocky side of the bluff. Ned unstrapped the picnic basket from his bike, and he and Nancy made their way down to join the others at the bottom of the steps.

"Let's go over to that side of the beach," Katie said, pointing away from the sea lion nursery. "There's a natural stone picnic table over there."

Katie led them to a large rock with a flat top. Around it boulders served as stools and benches.

"I love this," Nancy said. "It feels so private." The stretch of beach felt like a large room. The bluff reached up about fifteen feet behind them. Beside them, a tower of rock climbed higher than the bluff. About one-third of the rock was anchored in the sandy beach. The rest rose up from the ocean.

The rock was covered with thousands of pale gray– and dark blue–striped shells. They looked as if they had been glued on to the rock in a mixed-up jumble. Bess reached out and touched one of the shells. "What are these?" she asked.

"Mussels," Katie answered, taking paper plates and napkins out of her backpack. "That whole rock's just one big mussel bed."

"Hey, look at this," George called out. She was crouched at the edge of the water near another, smaller boulder.

Nancy and Ned joined her to look down into a small pool of water, completely surrounded by sand and rock. "A tide pool," Nancy said, leaning down to get a closer look. It was a miniature ocean, alive with small fish and sea cucumbers. A starfish sprawled across an underwater ledge. Crabs scurried across the shells lining the pool's bottom, and flowerlike sea urchins fluttered just beneath the water's surface.

"It's so beautiful here," Bess said. "We've got mountains behind us, the ocean in front of us."

"Yeah," George said, unwrapping a sandwich, "mountain biking behind us, sea kayaking in front of

5

us." She turned to Katie. "So, when does the training begin? Ned and I are eager to get into our cockpits and start paddling."

"Jenna is due tomorrow," Katie answered, taking a bite from a juicy peach. "Jenna Deblin. George, I think you met her at a world trials once. She's coming down from Seattle to train with us."

"Don't forget the whale watching," Bess reminded them. "That's what *I'm* here for."

"Don't worry," Katie told her with a smile. "We'll definitely get some of that in. In fact, you may be my last whale watchers. I'm thinking about closing the business."

"What do you mean?" Nancy asked, opening a soda. "Is the business not as much fun as you'd thought it would be?"

"Actually, it's wonderful," Katie said, gazing down at the water drifting over the sand. "I'm not busy all the time—just during the migrations, so it gives me plenty of time to kayak. And I like the tourists who come to see the whales—it's fun meeting people from all over."

"So, what's the problem?" Ned asked. "Why are you thinking about closing up shop?"

Katie reached into a bag for a few chips, stared at them, then dropped them one by one onto her plate. For a minute Nancy thought the young woman was going to cry. Then Katie surprised her. She looked up, her dark eyes fiery with anger. "Because I may not have any choice, that's why!"

6

she said, her words popping like little explosions in the air.

"Someone's trying to force me out of business," she continued. "I've gotten anonymous notes, threatening phone calls. It's driving me nuts." She pulled her head up high. "But I just don't want to throw in the towel. I want to hold on as long as I can. Maybe they'll give up."

"Who?" Nancy asked. "Who do you think is doing it?"

"And why?" Bess added.

"I don't know for sure," Katie said. "This is a very small town. It's been a sleepy little fishing village for over a century."

"That means many generations of fishermen," Nancy guessed. "And they're pretty protective of their territory, I'll bet."

"You've got it," Katie said with a nod. "They believe they've inherited these waters for their family trade, and they're not thrilled to be sharing their territory with an outsider like me. After all, I've only been here five years. I'm still an alien. I might as well have dropped from Mars, as far as the locals are concerned."

"Why should they care?" Ned asked. "You're not fishing. You're not in competition with them."

"I know, but they think I'm interfering anyway," Katie said. "They think taking a boat of tourists out for a day's excursion disrupts the waters and cuts down on their catch." She squared her shoulders. "And it might," she said. "But I've got just as much right to those waters as they do. I live here, too."

"And you should be able to make a living, too," Bess said, placing an arm around Katie's shoulders.

"It seems to me that dozens of whales swimming through the waters makes a disruption anyway," George said. "Adding a whale-watching excursion to the mix shouldn't make that much difference."

"Right," Ned agreed. "After all, it's only a few months a year. That's not too much to ask."

"I expect it's more than just the excursions," Nancy said. "It's the whole idea of tourists coming into town, strangers wandering around, cars parked everywhere. Do you suspect anyone in particular?"

"Well, there's a third-generation local named Holt Scotto," Katie answered. "He's sort of the leader of the fishermen. He has the biggest boat and seems to be the one who makes all the decisions. If he's not causing the trouble I'm having, he has to know about it and who's responsible."

"Nancy can help," George said. "Remember, I told you she's a world-famous detective. I'm sure she'd be happy to look into it for you, wouldn't you, Nancy?"

Nancy smiled at Katie and George, saying, "Sure, I could—"

"No, thank you," Katie said, cutting Nancy off. "I appreciate it, but I'd rather figure it out for myself," she added with a tight smile. "I think I can win these guys over eventually." She started gathering up soda cans and trash. "Well, we need to get back home if we're going to beat the fog and go on a sunset cruise."

As they cleaned up the area, Nancy noticed the huge bank of fog over the water. While they were eating, it had hung in the distance, an enormous gray cloud that rested on the ocean, swallowing up the horizon. Now it was moving slowly toward them.

Katie followed Nancy's gaze. As if reading her thoughts, Katie said, "I love the fog. It's so mysterious. It will touch the shore by nighttime and crawl clear into the hills."

"It looks so solid from here," Bess said. "Almost like a silver wall."

"But when you're in it, it's just wisps," Katie murmured. "One second you can see for miles, the next you see nothing but fog."

Nancy felt a chill shimmy down her back. What was that, she wondered. She reached for her sweatshirt. The sun's going down, she assured herself. It's getting cooler. But she couldn't shake the odd feeling. There's something funny going on here, she thought. I wonder what we're getting into.

On the bike ride back to Katie's, Nancy thought about her new friend's predicament. She wished Katie would accept her help. Nancy decided to keep her eyes and ears open, just in case.

When they got back to Katie's house, they put

their bikes and the picnic stuff away. After freshening up and grabbing sweaters, they followed Katie onto a long finger of land stretching into the ocean. There, in a boathouse, Katie's boat, the *Ripper,* bounced on the gently rippling tide.

Katie led them up the ramp to the deck, which was partly open and partly enclosed with windows along the sides. She stopped with a gasp when she stepped on deck. "Look what they did!" she yelled. "They trashed her!"

2

Open Up!

Nancy ran up the ramp and shuddered as she glanced around the deck of the *Ripper.* Cushions were thrown on the floor, foam stuffing spilling out of their slashed green- and white-striped covers. Sunshades had been ripped from their hardware, leaving ugly gashes in the wooden window casings. Coils of heavy rope had been hacked into fraying pieces.

Katie ran across the deck and down the steps to the cabin. Nancy and Ned followed her. Nancy stepped gingerly over the mess in the galley. Cupboards were splintered, with the remaining pieces dangling from broken hinges. Napkins, spoons, and bananas littered the floor.

Leaning against the galley wall, Katie slowly sank

11

to the floor. "This must have happened while we were on our picnic," she said. "I came down here just before we left. How could they do this?" she asked, her eyes filling with tears. "Hang-up phone calls are one thing, but this . . ."

Bess and George crowded into the small space. "I'm so sorry, Katie," George said, going over to comfort her friend. "Please let Nancy help. I told you before. She's a real ace as a detective."

"She's solved cases all over the world," Ned added, smiling fondly at Nancy, then at Katie. "I know she can figure this one out."

"And we'll all help!" Bess declared. "We'll find out who's doing this and put an end to it, won't we, Nancy?"

"I'd be glad to look into it," Nancy said. She liked Katie and thought her new friend was getting a bad deal.

"Okay, I believe you," Katie said. "Maybe I do need help. I'd love to have the opinion of someone from the outside on this. Someone who's more objective and not all emotional about everything."

"Well, you've got four someones right here," Bess said. "We'll get to the bottom of this."

Katie and George went back to the house to call the sheriff. Nancy, Ned, and Bess stayed to watch the boat. "Look around for clues," Nancy told the others, "but don't disturb anything."

Katie and George returned shortly. "Seabreak is

too small for its own police force," Katie told them. "I called Sheriff Harvey. He works this part of the county. He lives in the next town, but he'll be here soon."

While they all looked around, Nancy questioned Katie about the notes and phone calls but didn't learn anything that she thought could help. Katie said Sheriff Harvey had investigated, but there just weren't any clues to pursue. He talked to Holt Scotto and some of the other Seabreak fishermen, but they all claimed to know nothing.

"What's this?" Nancy wondered, crouching to get a better look. It was the torn fragment of what looked like a business card that had fallen under one of the window seats. The words "Lone Motel" were printed on it in fancy type. The line below read "way 1." In the corner, someone had handwritten the number 7 in ink.

"Do you think that was dropped by one of the vandals?" Bess asked.

"As I said before, I'm not the best housekeeper in the world," Katie said. "But I'm better than this," she added with a wry smile and a sweep of her arm. "That piece of paper could have been here for months, dropped by one of my whale watchers."

"When was the last time you did a real cleaning job on this place?" Nancy asked. "And how many people have been on board since?"

"Oh, probably three weeks," Katie said. "I've had

13

a few nearly full boats since then—maybe thirty or forty people. I can find out exactly when I check my records."

"That means fingerprinting's probably not going to be much help," Ned concluded. "Right, Nancy?"

"You're probably right," Nancy said. She drew a copy of the business card fragment in a small notebook she carried in her jeans pocket.

When Sheriff Harvey arrived, Katie introduced him to the others, briefly mentioning Nancy's reputation as a detective. He gave Nancy a curious smile.

Nancy pointed out the business card fragment, which he picked up with a tissue and pocketed. He agreed that fingerprinting would probably not be much help, but took a few impressions from the places where the damage was the greatest.

"It's got to be Scotto or some of his buddies," Katie told the sheriff. "Who else would do this?"

"I'll talk to them again, Ms. Firestone," Sheriff Harvey said, reassuring her. "And I'll check out these prints. But it could have just been some kids up from the city, looking for trouble. We've had a few reports up and down the coast about similar incidents. Maybe some of these prints will match the ones taken from the other boats and cottages that have been vandalized. Meanwhile, you be sure to let me know if anything else happens."

As he started to leave the boat, he turned. "All of

you be careful—and don't take it on yourselves to be snooping around," he said, looking at Nancy.

After the sheriff left, George offered to help Katie clean up the boat.

"I need to go into town to pick up a few things I forgot to pack," Bess said. "Then I'll come back and help."

"I'll drive you in," Nancy said. "I want to look around a little anyway, while the trail is still fresh."

"You two aren't going into enemy territory without me," Ned insisted, taking Nancy's hand.

"Thanks for all the help with the cleanup," George said sarcastically, her mouth twisted into a half-smile.

"Let them go," Katie said. "From what you've said, Nancy is the best. Let her get to work."

"I'm just kidding," George said, grinning. "But remember what the sheriff said," she warned her friends. "Be careful."

Seabreak was one of the tiny towns dotting the coastal bluffs from San Francisco north to the Oregon border. It had old wood-frame houses with small lawns, a tiny bakery, a bare-essentials grocery store. There were no tourist souvenir shops—not even a gas station.

"Katie was right," Bess murmured. "This is a sleepy little town."

There was a natural wharf created by a rocky shoal along the shore. A long pier jutted out from the harbor. Several fishing boats bobbed in the water along the pier. The sun had set, but the sky still glowed a pale peach color. Thin spikes of fog filled the air.

An old-fashioned diner perched on the edge of the bluff above the wharf. Ned parked the car in the diner parking lot. Nancy led Bess and Ned down the rickety wooden-plank steps to the shore. Then they strolled along the pier to a string of fishing boats. As they walked closer, they could see the bustling activity of the boat owners.

One fisherman noticed Nancy and her friends and stepped onto the pier from his small boat. "Can I help ya?" he asked.

"No," Nancy said quickly. "We're just enjoying the sunset. It's a beautiful evening. Are you going to do some night fishing?"

The man stared at Nancy. His eyes seemed not to blink at all. She tried to match him, locking into his gaze. When he finally spoke, she realized she'd been holding her breath.

"Yep," he said. "Say, you're not locals. Are you up from the city. Tourists, maybe?"

"We're visiting a friend," Nancy said, smiling. "One of your neighbors. You probably know her— Katie Firestone?"

The man's eyelids lowered a little as he looked from Nancy to Ned to Bess, and then back to Nancy.

"Yes, I know her," he said slowly. "The whale watcher."

"Well, actually, we're here to do some sea kayak training with her," Nancy said. "Right, Ned?" She turned to him, giving him the cue to join in the conversation.

"That's right," Ned said, taking a step forward. "Hi. I'm Ned Nickerson." He held out his hand.

"Nice to meet ya," the man said. He shook Ned's hand but didn't offer his name.

"I'm really looking forward to the sea kayaking," Ned added, giving the fisherman one of his classic broad smiles. "Katie's a world-class athlete, you know," Ned continued. "Seabreak is lucky to have such a winner living here."

"Lucky, hmmm?" the man said. "Well, some people have different views of luck than others. What's good luck to some might be bad luck to others. Enjoy your stay—but be careful of the sneakers."

Nancy looked down at her shoes, and then looked back. But the fisherman had disappeared into his boat.

"Let's go back to that diner," Nancy said, looking up at the small building on the bluff above them.

There were only a few people in the diner. When the waitress brought over the suppers they ordered, Nancy asked her a few questions. But the young woman seemed suspicious and unwilling to talk.

Finally Nancy, Ned, and Bess went back to the inn where they were staying.

"I wish we were staying at Katie's with George," Bess said when they got into the room she was sharing with Nancy. "The inn is nice, but it would be more fun to kick around that cool house."

"She doesn't really have the space for all of us," Nancy reminded Bess. "Especially with the other sea kayaker coming in tomorrow."

"Besides, Katie's house is only about a mile down the road," Ned added. "And she said we can come and go any time we want. I intend to take her up on that. I'm showing up early tomorrow morning to see if I can't talk her into some kayaking."

"She told us to come over for breakfast about eight-thirty or nine," Nancy reminded him.

"Great—I'll meet you downstairs," Ned said. "Eight-fifteen."

Ned left for his room. Nancy looked out the window, thinking about the evening's investigation.

"I wonder how the boat cleanup went," Bess said, plunking down on the bed by the little fireplace. "I wonder if Katie and George found any more clues."

"I doubt it." Nancy sank into a plush green chair. "I'm sure George would have called if they had." She pulled the copy of the business card fragment from her pocket and studied it for a moment.

"Do you really think that's anything, Nancy?"

18

Bess asked. "As Katie said, it could have been dropped by any one of dozens of people."

"I know," Nancy agreed, "but right now it's all we've—"

"Hey!" A booming voice exploded like a cannon from the hall outside their door.

Nancy's words caught in her throat as Bess ran to her side, trembling. Nancy's pulse seemed to beat in rhythm to the pounding on the door, and the whole room seemed to shake. "Hey!" the man yelled again. "Are you in there? Open this door. *Now.*"

3

The Tail Is Turned

"Open up!" the man yelled again, beating hard on the door. "I want to talk to you."

Bess looked at Nancy, her eyes wide with apprehension. "Who could that be?" she whispered. "Nancy! What'll we do?"

Nancy felt a shudder tumble through her as she held her hand up to Bess. As she walked toward the door, she heard Ned's voice in the hall.

"Cool down," Ned said from the other side of the door. "Who are you? What do you want?"

"I'm Holt Scotto, that's who." The words blasted through the door. Nancy reached for the knob and opened the door.

Scotto was tall, with short hair bleached straw

20

blond by the sun and a small gold hoop in one ear. His eyes were narrowed as he stared at Nancy.

Ned stepped between them in the doorway. With one sweep of his beefy arm, Scotto pushed Ned aside and continued to glare at Nancy.

"You're the one asking questions at the diner and down at the pier," Scotto said to Nancy. "Who are you? What do you want?"

"I'm Nancy Drew, a friend of Katie Firestone," Nancy said.

"So that's it," Scotto said. "I might have known."

"Why don't you come in," Nancy said. "We can talk in the room. There's no point in disturbing the other guests."

"I can say my piece right here," Scotto declared. "How come you're snooping around town? What's Firestone got to do with you?"

"Her boat was vandalized earlier today," Nancy said. From the corner of her eye, she could see Mrs. Oprey, the innkeeper, hurrying down the hall. "I thought maybe one of the fishermen saw something from a boat as he went in or out of the harbor," Nancy said.

"So somebody trashed her boat, hmm?" Scotto said with a snort. "Well, I know what happens next. I get hassled by the sheriff. That's what always happens when Little Miss Katie has a problem." His face was dark red—partly from the sun, Nancy guessed, but not completely. He seemed very angry.

"Holt Scotto, you get out of my inn," Mrs. Oprey said. "Stop causing such a ruckus or I will call the sheriff on you. You're bothering my other guests. Now, get!"

"Look, Mr. Scotto, perhaps the sheriff contacts you because you seem to be the town leader," Nancy said in a soothing voice. "It's clear that the other fishermen look up to you. Sheriff Harvey probably figures there's nothing that happens around here that you don't know about."

"You're pretty smooth, but I'm not buying it," Scott said. His mouth clenched tight above his square jaw. "You quit poking around. I'm not warning you again. If you mess with me, you'll be sorry."

"That does it," Ned said, stepping toward Scotto. "Back off."

For a moment it looked as if Scotto might hit Ned, but Ned folded his arms across his chest and gave the intruder a fierce look.

Scotto took a half-step back. Then, with one last warning glare at Nancy, he stalked away.

"Are you okay?" Ned asked Nancy. "Do you want me to follow him out? Make sure he leaves?"

"Maybe we *should* call Sheriff Harvey," Bess added, her voice low.

"I'm so sorry," Mrs. Oprey said. "I wouldn't be too worried about Holt. He's got a terrible temper, but his bark's worse than his bite, as they say. He wouldn't really hurt anyone, he's just kind of private.

Doesn't like people nosing into his affairs." She gave Nancy and the others a warm smile. "Can I get you some tea?"

"Nothing for me, thanks," Bess said. "My nerves are jangling enough."

"Thanks, Mrs. Oprey, we're fine," Nancy said. The innkeeper bustled off to soothe other guests who had gathered in the hall.

"That guy was creepy," Bess said, and Ned stepped in and closed the door. "Nancy, are you sure there isn't something we can do?"

"I don't think we need to follow him or call the sheriff," Nancy answered.

"But he threatened you," Bess protested.

"Not with anything specific," Nancy said. "And he didn't lay a hand on any of us. He just made a lot of noise. If Mrs. Oprey doesn't want to charge him for disturbing the peace, we really don't have much of a claim. If he does try something later, at least we'll have a lot of witnesses to tonight's threats."

"Well, Mrs. Oprey might think Scotto's just a big blowhard," Ned said, "but I'm not so sure."

"I'm going to call George and tell her what happened," Bess said. She settled down at the little desk and made her call.

"We really didn't get much information on our trip into town," Nancy said, and pulled out her drawing of the business card fragment.

"You really think that could be something, don't you," Ned said, nodding at the fragment.

"I do," Nancy said. "I know Katie thought it could have been dropped by one of her whale watchers, but it seems too crisp and clean to have been there very long."

"You're right," Ned said. "It really doesn't look like it's been sitting around a damp boat for a while."

"If it was dropped by someone who vandalized Katie's boat, then that person may be staying in a motel," Nancy pointed out. "That would seem to rule out a local culprit."

She checked the telephone book. "There's only one place around here that could possibly match this business card," she said, pointing to the name. "The Abalone Motel. It's about ten miles down the coast road. I think I'll run down there tomorrow."

"Count me out," Ned said. "I promised to help rehab the boat."

"I'll go," Bess said, joining them after her phone call.

"Just don't forget breakfast at Katie's," Ned said, walking to the door. "Tomorrow morning, lobby downstairs, eight-fifteen," Ned reminded them as he left to go to his room.

After he left, Bess and Nancy talked a little until they fell asleep.

* * *

24

Over eggs and muffins at Katie's the next morning, they talked about the investigation in town and confrontation with Holt Scotto.

"That fisherman on the pier said the strangest thing," Bess reported. "He gave us a goofy warning, saying to enjoy our stay but be careful of sneakers. What do you suppose he meant?"

"I know exactly what he meant," Katie said. "There are these weird waves along this stretch of the coast. They're called sneaker waves. They seem to come out of nowhere—with no warning. Hikers and shell collectors get swept right out to sea by them."

"Are you serious?" Ned asked.

"Deadly serious," Katie said. "The locals have a slogan they always tell visitors: stay alert, keep escape routes in mind, and never turn your back on the ocean."

"So how come you never told us about that yesterday when we were at the beach?" George said, poking her friend in the side with her elbow.

"Because we were in a cove protected by those huge rock formations," Katie pointed out. "By the time the waves get to the shore there, they've been cut down by the rocks."

"Those rocks were something," Bess said. "They're so huge and rise right out of the ocean."

"Technically, they're called sea stacks, or just stacks," Katie said. "And you haven't seen anything yet. Wait till we go to the place I want to use for kayak training. It has whole hills of rock coming up out of the water. One even has grass and wildflowers growing on top of it. There are several that are hollowed out like tunnels—and huge. Big enough to take my boat through."

"They sound like fun to explore," George said.

"You have to be careful, though," Katie warned. "There are sea caves, which are huge hollowed-out rock formations, there also. They're just like land caves, except the floor is the water. They can be pretty spooky inside—just like any cave."

"Speaking of training," Ned said, finishing his eggs. "I'm ready!"

"I've still got a lot of work to do on the boat," Katie said.

"It's a real mess," George added. "They even tampered with the engine."

"I've got to get it fixed," Katie said. "It's my income, and I need—"

The ringing phone interrupted her. From where they sat, Nancy and the others could hear Katie's end of the conversation.

"Well, hello, Mr. Jason," Katie said. "I wondered whether you'd be calling again. It's been at least three days since I heard from you." Nancy could hear the sarcasm in Katie's voice.

"No, I haven't changed my mind," Katie said firmly. "I like my business just the way it is. I intend to stay independent." There was a brief silence while Katie listened to her caller. "No way, Mr. Jason. All right . . . Andy. There's no need to call me anymore. My decision is final. Thanks."

Katie hung up the phone and returned to the table. "Andy Jason," she told the others. "He owns a small fleet of whale-watching excursion boats up and down the coast. He's been trying to get me to shut down my business and go to work for him—or at least to buy into one of his franchises."

"But you don't want to?" George asked.

"No way," Katie said. "Andy Jason's pretty aggressive, though. Doesn't like anyone to tell him no. I think he wants all the whale-watching business from San Francisco to Oregon."

"Did you ever think that he might be doing all this bad stuff to you?" George asked. "It's one way to get rid of the competition."

"George has a point, Katie," Nancy said.

"I did catch him snooping around my boat once, but I don't know. Well, if he's trying to drum me out of business, it won't work," Katie announced. "I'll never work for Andy Jason. I like being my own boss because I get to decide when I take tourists out and when I take a day off for kayaking."

"Speaking of kayaking," Ned repeated.

"Definitely a one-track mind," Nancy groaned.

"I was going to say that I could help you with the boat repairs this morning, Katie," Ned offered. "I figure the sooner we get the *Ripper* seaworthy, the sooner we can climb into the kayak cockpits."

"Wonderful," Katie replied. "How about you, George. Ready for more work?"

"I'm in for the duration," George said with a lopsided grin.

"I'm going to the Abalone Motel to check it out," Nancy said. "But then I'll report for duty."

"I'll go keep Nancy company," Bess said, "but after that, you can count on me, too."

"With all this help, we're bound to be finished soon," Katie said. "Thanks a lot, guys."

It was nearly noon by the time Nancy and Bess finally left for their drive down the coast. It was a beautiful day. Nancy and Bess had both grabbed sweatshirts, but so far T-shirts and jeans were all they had needed in the warm late-January sun. Twice Nancy pulled off onto a scenic overlook so Bess could snap a photo of the majestic hills and sea.

"All I know is—" Bess started to say, interrupting herself when she glanced at Nancy. "What is it?" she asked. "What do you see?"

Bess started to turn around, but Nancy stopped her. "No, don't look out the back." Nancy stared into the rearview mirror.

"You're scaring me, Nan," Bess whispered. She hunched down a little in her seat, then said, "Come on, tell me. What are you looking at? Who is it?" Bess repeated. "Is it Holt Scotto?"

"I'm not sure," Nancy answered. "I'm not even sure he's following us. But when I slow down, he slows down. When I drive faster, he speeds up, too."

Nancy accelerated up a hill. As she began her descent on the other side, she realized that her car and the one following were the only two on the road for as far as she could see. She glanced at the other car in her mirror. It was a rusty old red Mustang, and it was barreling down the hill toward her.

"He's coming faster," Nancy said. She felt her breathing speed up, too. She pressed down on the accelerator pedal a little harder.

She looked up again. The car was charging toward her, filling her rearview mirror.

4

Lights Out

The reflection in Nancy's rearview mirror grew larger as the car behind them moved faster.

"He's not going to stop," Nancy told Bess. "I've got to get out of the way."

With no warning, Nancy turned onto a dirt road leading up into a canyon. She drove as fast as she could up the hilly narrow road, checking her rearview mirror frequently. When she came to another road branching to the right, she turned onto it.

After checking her mirror, she slowed to a stop.

Bess turned around to check out the back window. "Did he follow us?"

"I don't think so," Nancy said. "I don't think he

turned off the coast road, and he definitely wasn't back there to see me take this offshoot."

They waited a few minutes, then Nancy backed carefully off the side road on to the main canyon two-lane. Slowly she headed back down to the coast road. She scanned both ways a long time before finally pulling out onto it and driving south toward the Abalone Motel.

As she drove, she checked the cars along the way, but saw nothing like the rusty red Mustang that had been following them earlier.

Finally they reached the motel, and within minutes Nancy knew the trip had been for nothing. She held the business card for the Abalone Motel in one hand and the drawing of the card scrap she had found on Katie's boat in the other. "Look," she showed Bess. "They don't match."

Nancy couldn't keep the disappointment out of her voice. This was the one possible physical clue they had—and it was a dead end.

"Now what?" Bess asked, her pale eyebrows squinched into a frown.

"Back to the *Ripper*," Nancy said with a sigh. As they left the motel, she noticed a poster for Andy Jason's whale-watching excursions. "Looks as if he has an office about twenty miles south of here," she told Bess. "Let's take a look."

The winding two-lane road stayed pretty close to the coast, diverting once in a while to run through a small town or by a tiny shopping district. Finally they came to a boat-shaped building topped with a colorful sign: See Migrating Whales Up Close! the sign read. Finest Fleet Afloat! Andy Jason, Owner.

"Grab your camera, Bess," Nancy said. They stepped inside the building. The nautical theme was carried throughout the interior. A huge anchor lay like a modern sculpture in the center of the room. A receptionist sat at a desk ringed with life preservers hung from a thick white rope. "May I help you?" the young woman asked with a toothy smile.

"I hope so," Nancy answered. "Is Mr. Jason in, by any chance?"

"Are you interested in one of our excursions?" the young girl asked. "I can help you with reservations or information."

"Actually, I'd like to speak with Mr. Jason," Nancy said. "I'm starting a small weekly newspaper, the *Canyon Courier*. I'm interviewing local businesspeople for the first issue. Mr. Jason is certainly a mover and shaker in this area, and he should be in the premiere issue, don't you think? I realize I should have called to make an appointment, but starting a paper is just so crazy. There are a million things to do. My photographer and I were driving by and we thought we'd stop. If Mr. Jason is in, we could do the interview right now."

The young girl's eyes sparkled with excitement.

"Oh, absolutely," she said. "Just wait right here. Don't move. I'll see if Mr. Jason is available."

Nancy fished in her bag for the notebook and pen she always carried. Bess checked her camera. "I've got two shots left," she murmured to Nancy.

"Make it look good," Nancy whispered as the young receptionist bustled back into the room. She was followed by a slim man in a navy blazer with brass buttons. He looked as if he was in his mid-thirties.

"So who have we here?" the man asked, holding out his right hand. "I'm Andy Jason. I understand you want to talk to me." He was of medium height, with brown hair and a neatly trimmed beard and mustache.

"I'm Linnie Lowell," Nancy said, shaking his hand. "Nice to meet you. I'm the publisher of the *Canyon Courier*. This is my photographer, Jane Cloud."

Bess stepped forward with a big smile and shook Jason's hand.

"If you have some time now, Mr. Jason," Nancy said, "I'd love to interview you for a feature I'm doing on the business leaders of this area."

"Only if you'll call me Andy," Jason said, giving Nancy an admiring glance. "After all, it sounds as if you're going to be a business leader around here yourself. We're almost colleagues." He gestured toward his office. "Can I get either of you anything? How about a soda? I'm having one."

"Nothing for me, thanks," Nancy said. "If I could just ask you a few questions, Mr. Jason—I'm sorry—

Andy." While Nancy talked, Bess walked slowly around the room, aiming her camera, looking through the viewfinder, and checking the angle of the sunlight as it flowed through the window. She perfectly imitated a professional photographer lining up a shot.

"Well, Mr. Jason—Andy," Nancy began, "how long have you been offering whale-watching excursions in this area?"

While Andy Jason answered Nancy's steady questions, she studied him. He seemed open and friendly.

"I'm in the process of locating here right now," Nancy said. "Are you the only whale-watching business in this area?"

"The only one that counts," Andy said. His smile faded and Nancy noticed a sudden abrupt tone in his voice.

"So you do have competition," Nancy said, egging him on.

"Not really," Andy said. "There's one small outfit north of here—owned by a young woman. But she won't be around much longer." He looked out the window and seemed lost in thought for a moment.

"Really?" Nancy asked. "Is she going out of business?"

"One way or the other," Andy muttered in a low voice. Then he seemed to recover his friendly attitude and smiled quickly at Nancy. "I've made the young lady an offer, and I hope she'll be coming to work for me."

"Then you will be *the* whale-watching excursion around here," Nancy concluded.

"Absolutely," Andy replied. Nancy heard a tough edge in his voice and knew he was very determined.

After several more questions, Bess took a couple of photos, and she and Nancy left.

"What happens when he finds out we're not journalists named Linnie and Jane?" Bess asked.

"I told him the paper was just getting started and the first issue would come out in two months. By then he'll probably have forgotten about it."

"At least we'll be gone." Bess laughed. "I didn't like the way he talked about Katie. It sounded kind of creepy. Maybe George was right, and Andy's the one who's been causing all the trouble."

"Maybe," Nancy agreed.

After a quick lunch Nancy started the drive back up the coast to Seabreak. They had driven only a few miles when Bess suddenly asked Nancy to stop.

"Oh, look!" Bess exclaimed, pointing out the front window. "Look at that great old lighthouse. Let's go take a look, Nancy. Just for a minute."

Nancy peered down the narrow road leading to the shore and the long rock jetty with the lighthouse at the end. "We can take a few minutes," she said, turning the car. "Well, look at that," she added, pointing to a car parked at the bottom of the narrow, steep road. It was the rusty red Mustang.

Nancy parked the car and they walked onto an old boardwalk of abandoned shops. She and Bess took a closer look at the Mustang. It was locked, and the interior was a mess of papers, ropes, tools, and three pairs of boots. Nancy wrote the license plate number in her notebook.

A few other cars were parked here, too. Nancy saw a family collecting shells down the beach. They were about a hundred yards away—as far away as the length of a fooball field. There was no one else in sight. She hurried to catch up with Bess, who had started toward the old lighthouse. As Nancy picked her way along the rocks to the end of the long jetty, she felt as if she and Bess were completely alone.

They finally arrived at the tall structure, which was in pretty bad shape. The paint was faded and peeling. Part of a metal staircase that wound around the outside of the lighthouse had pulled away and drooped precariously above them.

The lighthouse was surrounded by a metal fence. Nancy could tell that it had been breached by earlier trespassers.

"Come on," Bess said. She ducked under a huge yellow sign reading Keep Out, through a large hole in the fence, and up to the lighthouse door. All her senses on alert, Nancy followed quickly.

The lighthouse door was ajar. The whining scrape

of the rust brown hinges sent a shiver through her as she pulled it open. She shook it off and stepped into a large round room.

It took a minute for Nancy's eyes to adjust to the dim light, but when they did she saw one row of windows halfway up the building and another at the top. The light from these filtered down to the lighthouse floor through a thick layer of dust.

Bess seemed more cautious inside the lighthouse. "Whoa!" she exclaimed, frantically grasping at cobwebs in her hair. "I don't know what's ickier. The live things we might run into, or the dead thing that's making that awful smell."

"I think it's rotting seaweed or mold or something," Nancy said. "Doesn't look like there's been anyone in here for a while."

"I hope you're right," Bess mumbled. She seemed to hang back, waiting for Nancy to take the lead.

"Hey, you're the one who wanted to explore," Nancy said. "Let's do it."

Nancy stepped carefully through the piles of newspapers, driftwood, and other debris littering the floor of the lighthouse. "Hmmm, I might have spoken too soon," Nancy said, stopping suddenly.

"What do you mean?" Bess asked. She was following so closely, she bumped into Nancy.

"I'm not sure." Nancy's voice was lowered almost to a whisper. She crouched and looked closely, flashing her penlight around the floor. "It looks as if someone has walked through here. Look—damp splotches about the size of a large foot. Like someone tramped through here in wet boots."

"Recently?" Bess asked, her voice high. "Where do the steps lead?"

"They sort of start here and they seem to be jumbled, as if someone turned several times and then just stopped over here." Nancy pointed out a group of several damp smudges on the old wooden floor.

There was a small closet about a foot from the last smudge. A low shuffling sound rustled from under the door. Nancy picked up a piece of driftwood and crept to the closet door. As she neared it, the sound behind the door became louder, more urgent. Holding the driftwood firmly with one hand, she grasped the knob with the other.

Nancy hesitated a moment, her hand on the knob. Bess stood close behind her, holding a large rock she had found on the lighthouse floor.

Raising the driftwood high over her shoulder, Nancy turned the knob and yanked open the door.

5

The Shadow in the Cypresses

With a loud rustle of its wings, a seagull flapped out
of the closet. Startled, Nancy and Bess jumped back
as the gull flew past them and out the front door of
the lighthouse.

Adrenaline coursed through Nancy's body, and
she gulped.

"Yikes!" Bess finally cried. "I was really scared for a
minute." She giggled. "When that thing flew out—"
She stopped for a moment to gasp in more air.

"It *was* pretty amazing," Nancy agreed. "I had no
idea what was making that noise."

"That gull didn't seem to be injured or anything,"
Bess added. "Just locked in."

"Yeah," Nancy said, her voice lower. "And by

whom? It didn't seem to be weak or starving—and obviously hadn't been trapped for very long."

"You're saying it was locked in pretty recently?" Bess asked.

"Maybe *very* recently," Nancy said, looking around the room.

"Maybe we should leave," Bess said. "After all, the sign did say Keep Out."

"Well, we're in here now. Let's check out that view. Come on—there's the staircase."

It took them a while to climb to the top of the tower, the equivalent of six flights of stairs. Nancy felt a little giddy as they wound around and around the open metal staircase.

When they reached the top, they stopped for a minute to catch their breath. Bess started giggling again and couldn't seem to stop. "Don't get me started," Nancy said, laughing.

"When that gull flew out, my heart absolutely stopped," Bess sputtered.

"Amazing how fast we can move when we're motivated, right?" Nancy stepped from the tiny stair landing out into the small room that surrounded the staircase.

"Someone was in here, though," Nancy said. "Probably today. Those smudges were still damp, and they're too big to have been made by the gull. And did you notice the doorknob?"

"No. What do you mean?"

"The doorknob was clean," Nancy answered. "No dust. Someone had opened it recently."

Bess's giggling stopped and a worried frown scrunched up her face. "But it could have been anybody, right? Someone just like us. Someone who wanted to see this gorgeous view."

"Probably," Nancy answered, walking along the worn planks of flooring. The top half of the room was a wall of windows. "Wow! I feel like I can see all the way to Katie's, more than twenty miles away."

"It's so beautiful," Bess responded. "It really was worth the climb."

For the first few miles along the shore rounded hills of golden grasses gently tumbled into the sea. Farther north, the bluffs angled sharply down into the blue-green water. Stacks of rock shot up through the waves in formations that reminded Nancy of the landscapes in sci-fi movies.

Nancy checked her watch. "We'd better get back. The others probably expected us before now."

As she turned to go back to the staircase landing, Nancy saw a quick flash of yellow in the corner of her eye. She turned to see someone in a yellow rain jacket running away from the lighthouse along the jetty rocks. The person seemed surefooted, at home racing along the treacherous rocks.

"Someone *was* here recently," Bess said, looking over Nancy's shoulder at the person in the flapping yellow jacket.

Nancy bolted for the staircase and raced down the winding stairs, holding tightly to the railing. She wanted her feet to move fast, but she knew one misstep could send her into a free fall.

Nancy and Bess finally reached the bottom of the staircase and the wooden floor. Nancy ran to the lighthouse door and pulled. It didn't budge.

Bess ran up behind her. "Don't tell me, Nancy. Just don't say it."

"Okay, I won't tell you that we're locked in," Nancy said, jiggling the door. "Maybe it's just jammed. Come on, give me a shoulder."

They stood side by side, their shoulders against the door. Nancy counted to three, and they pushed as hard as they could. The door moved a little, but didn't open. They pushed again, and finally it opened enough for them to wiggle through.

Outside, a stack of rocks was leaning against the door.

"Do you think the person we saw running away did this?" Bess asked.

"Probably," Nancy replied. "And what do you bet he drives a red Mustang." When they reached their car, the Mustang was gone.

Nancy drove quickly to Katie's. By the time they got there, it was late afternoon.

"They must still be working on the boat," Nancy said when they found the house deserted. She and Bess headed immediately for the *Ripper.*

"Where have you been?" Ned asked as Nancy and Bess approached the boat. "We were about to file a Missing Persons report."

"It's been a strange day," Nancy said, sinking into one of the chairs on the deck. She and Bess told George, Ned, and Katie about their trip to the Abalone Motel, their meeting with Andy Jason, and their detour to the lighthouse.

"Let's call Sheriff Harvey," Katie suggested. "It sounds as if someone's stalking you, Nancy."

"I'd rather keep the sheriff out of this right now," Nancy said. She took a large gulp of the soda Katie handed her.

"Why, Nancy?" Katie said. "What if there's a connection between this guy and the one hassling me? Let's get him locked up and out of our hair."

"I know what the problem is," Bess offered. "We were trespassing at the lighthouse, right?"

"Right," Nancy said. "And we have no real proof anyone was following us—it's just a hunch."

"Okay, I'm going back to the house," Bess said, jumping up from her deck chair. "Katie, can I use your computer? I'm going to visit the motor vehicles department to see if I can find out whose Mustang that is."

"Sure," Katie replied.

Bess and George left. Nancy and Ned followed Katie belowdecks to help with the final cleanup. Then they made their way back to Katie's house.

"Ned was a big help with the engine repair," Katie told Nancy. "Now that the cleanup's finished, I'm hoping we can get some kayaking in tomorrow. Jenna should be getting in any time now, and if I know her, she'll be ready to rumble."

When they arrived at the house, they found Bess and George talking to a pretty young woman. She had an athletic body and medium blond hair that shone with pale streaks from the sun. She spoke fast, her words rippling out of her mouth.

"Jenna!" Katie cried. "You made it!" She clasped the young woman in a warm hug. "Did you have any trouble finding the place?"

"Not a bit. Your instructions were perfect—as always."

Katie introduced everyone. "Well, now we're really under the gun," she concluded. "Jenna's a champion competitor. Looks like we can't put off the training session any longer."

"Speaking of champs," George said, "tell them what you found out, Bess."

"Two words: Holt Scotto," Bess said triumphantly.

"The Mustang," Nancy murmured.

"I knew it!" Katie cried.

"That creep," Ned said through gritted teeth.

"Uh, hello," Jenna said. "You're all talking in code. Please fill in this poor Seattle alien."

"I'm through talking," Ned said, heading for the

door. "I'm going to find Scotto and deliver a few threats of my own—and maybe a few punches."

"I'm coming with you," Katie said. Her long face was flushed, and her graceful jaw clenched.

"Wait a minute, you two," Nancy called firmly. "You can't do that. It would be a huge mistake."

"But, Nancy," Bess said, "now we know it was Holt Scotto who locked us in the lighthouse."

"Actually, we only know that his car was parked near the lighthouse. We didn't see the driver close enough to identify. It could even have been a woman for all we know."

"But he threatened you last night," Katie protested.

"He told me not to mess with him," Nancy said.

"He followed you down the coast," George said. "He almost rammed into you."

"A car like his," Nancy corrected her. "I didn't see the license plate till later."

"This is so frustrating," Katie said. She leaned back against the wall and sank slowly to the floor.

"I know it is," Nancy said, crouching next to Katie. "Be patient. We'll keep an eye on him. And stay on guard, all of you. The whole town must know who we are by now."

Over dinner Nancy and the others told Jenna what had been happening to Katie. "I can't believe it," Jenna said, her large gray-blue eyes flashing with anger. "Are you sure the boat's okay now?"

45

"Sure," Ned said. "And Katie says she's taking us out tomorrow to an ideal kayak training place."

"It's pretty rough out there, but it'll make a great workout," Katie said. "And it has to be rough for Jenna," she told the others. "She's a real dynamo in the cockpit. The best team alternate we've got."

"Are you sure you have enough rigs for all of us?" Bess asked.

"I do," Katie answered. "Ned, George tells me you've done some sea kayaking already."

"A little," Ned said. "I've done a lot of white-water kayaying."

"Great!" Jenna said, flashing him a warm smile.

"Bess and I have done some river kayaking, too," Nancy said.

"But nothing real heavy," Bess pointed out quickly.

"Well, I'll do a refresher course for everyone who wants it before we go out," Katie said.

"How about a little biking to prep us for tomorrow?" Ned suggested.

"Good idea," Katie said. "Every time I get my bike on the road, it's free advertising. Nothing like flashing Firestone Whale Watching and my phone number to remind folks I'm in business—especially the ones who are fighting me on it."

"Count me out," Jenna said. "I'm too exhausted from the drive. In fact, I think I'll just finish unpacking the car and then crash. See you all tomorrow."

"You've got the room at the end of the hall," Katie said. "Just put your kayak and gear in the garage."

After dinner Nancy and her friends helped Katie clean up. "You know," Katie said. "I'm really behind on my paperwork. I think I'll take a pass on the bike ride, too, and just stay home to get it done. You guys will be okay without me, won't you?"

"Sure," George said. "We'll be fine."

"Great," Katie said, putting away the last clean dish. "Bess, the bike you rode yesterday needs cleaning—take my bike tonight. And everybody change to long pants and sweaters or jackets. It's going to get pretty chilly."

Nancy, Ned, Bess, and George changed clothes. Then they grabbed bikes and headed for the bluffs above the sea lion nursery. The sun had just set and the sky was the color of ripe canteloupe. The fog bank was still hundreds of yards away from shore. A few stars dangled in the glowing sky.

They dropped their bikes at the head of the wood steps leading down to the beach. George and Bess scrambled down to the water to check the tide pools before it got dark.

Nancy and Ned strolled along the bluff top on a little path worn by thousands of walkers and bikers before them. Ahead of them, the path led into the cypress grove known as the Cypress Cathedral. The trees were bent, windswept, and battered. Farther on they formed a tall arched room of pale gray trunks and dark green needles.

Nancy felt a chill of cool air rise up from the sea over the bluff and across the back of her neck. "Whooo," she said with a shiver. "Now I know how those trees feel."

"Where's your jacket?" Ned asked. "I thought you brought it."

"I did. It's with my bike. I didn't realize it would get so chilly so quickly."

"I'll get it for you," Ned said, loping back toward the bikes.

Nancy kept strolling slowly toward the Cypress Cathedral until she was actually in among the warped and twisted trunks. It became darker the farther she walked. But the air was warmer because the trees served as a windbreak.

Finally she heard Ned's footsteps behind her. "Guess what," she said, turning around. "I don't need my jacket in here, because—" The footsteps stopped, and she couldn't see Ned in the dim light.

"Ned?" It was so quiet in the grove. Another reason why they called it a cathedral, Nancy decided. "Ned. I know you're there."

But he wasn't. No one was.

"Must have been hearing things," Nancy mumbled unconvincingly to herself. She knew Ned would not tease her or try to scare her here. Not after all she'd been through that day.

48

She started forward again, slowly. Her ears strained to hear every possible crackling of a twig or shuffling of the sandy dirt.

Then she heard it again. It was definitely a footstep—several footsteps.

Nancy darted to the left, between two arched cypress trees. As she turned, she saw the silhouette of someone several yards from her. Nancy wove in and out of the tangled grove as fast as she could maneuver until she reached several braided trunks to use for cover. She could still hear footsteps, but they were farther away.

She was nearly out of breath, but she knew that any noise in this silent place would give away her hiding place. She clasped her hand across her mouth and sniffed precious dollops of air through her nose.

The footsteps stopped, and the sounds of her own breathing and a distant gull's cry were all she could hear.

6

A Break in the Action

A minute passed, and then another. Nancy waited breathlessly in her hiding place in the cypress grove. Finally she took a breath, and the aching in her lungs subsided.

Straining to pick up any sound from her stalker, she heard only voices in the distance.

Bess, George, and Ned were calling her from the bluff top. They sounded so far away, and she was a little disoriented from all her weaving in and out of the trees.

If I call back to them, will they hear me? she wondered. I'm sure the stalker will. Can Ned and the others get here before the stranger does?

She heard Ned and George repeat their call. The

footsteps inside the Cypress Cathedral started up again. This time, they weren't the nearly silent ones of someone sneaking up on her, as she had heard before. They were heavy footfalls, pounding toward her hiding place.

Nancy saw someone streak by her in a dark blur. The person ran so fast, she couldn't tell whether it was a man or a woman.

The footsteps grew fainter and fainter. Then, after a few minutes she heard a motor start up.

Cautiously, she emerged from her hiding place. There was no one in sight. She raced in the direction the person had run and came to an opening in the east side of the Cypress Cathedral. In the distance, she saw the dust of a vehicle heading down the road.

"Nancy! Nancy, where are you?" Ned's voice boomed from inside the cypress grove. "Stop playing games and get out here."

"I'm here, Ned," she called.

"What happened?" George asked as she, Bess, and Ned met Nancy under the arches of the trees. "Why didn't you answer when we called earlier?"

Quickly, Nancy told the others what had happened. The girls had seen nothing from their vantage point at the base of the bluff down on the beach.

"I didn't see anyone either," Ned said. "And I was on the trail the whole time, from the trees to the bikes and back again."

"Whoever it was could have come through the same way he—or she—exited," George said.

"And just hid in here, waiting for us to come in," Bess concluded. "Someone must have followed us out here."

"But aren't we jumping to conclusions again?" George asked. "Every time something weird happens, we assume it's a stalker or a threat. We don't really know that someone followed us here," she added. "Right, Nancy? It could just have been someone out for a sunset stroll on the bluffs or through the cypress grove. Maybe he—or she—was afraid of running into *you* in this dark place. What we see as menacing could have been fear or suspicion."

Nancy shook her head slowly, her brow pleated into a frown. "Actually, each one of these incidents by itself could be explained or excused as coincidence or accident or something else completely innocent. But when you add them up, it's just too much. Let's look around here. Maybe 'The Shadow' dropped a clue to help us out."

Armed with Nancy's and George's penlights, the four searched the Cypress Cathedral, but they found nothing.

"Let's get out of here," Bess said. "It's just about dark. And even with our lights it's going to be hard to see."

"Good idea," George agreed. "We need to get

some rest before we climb into the kayak cockpits tomorrow."

They picked up their bikes and started back. When they reached Seabreak, Nancy noticed a lot of cars parked on the bluff above the harbor. One of them was the rusty red Mustang.

"Looks like something's going on at the diner," Nancy said. "Let's stop for a soda."

Nancy and her friends locked their bikes in the bike rack and went into the diner. A woman was speaking at the front of the room. She looked about forty-five years old and had straight dark hair and glasses with gold wire frames.

"My name is Joan Kim," the woman announced as Nancy and the others walked across the room. "I own a small fleet of fishing boats up the coast. I've been told you are having some problems with a whale-watching business down here." She paced back and forth.

"I want you to know that we went through the same threat to our business that you are facing now," Joan Kim continued. "We managed to get the whale watching stopped and our waters kept free for fishing."

Nancy led Bess, George, and Ned to a booth just inside the door. No one spoke to them, but she recognized several of the fishermen and the waitress she had interviewed the night before. She scanned the room but did not see Holt Scotto.

"I'm sure most of you have heard of Andy Jason,"

Ms. Kim said after Nancy and her friends were seated. Bess poked Nancy's arm at the mention of Jason's name.

"He tried to bring whale-watching boats into my area," Ms. Kim continued. The woman smiled at the crowd. "But he didn't succeed."

"How'd you stop it?" someone asked from a stool at the counter.

"We banded together, that's how," Ms. Kim said. "We got all the fishermen together and launched a campaign to keep Andy Jason and all the whale-watching businesses out of our territory."

"What kind of a campaign are you talking about?" a woman asked from a table close to where Kim was standing.

"Nothing fatal," Ms. Kim added with a laugh. "And nothing strictly illegal. But there are things you can do to intimidate outsiders and discourage them from staying." As Joan Kim answered the question, the waitress came to Nancy's booth and quietly took their orders for sodas.

Nancy watched while the waitress went back behind the counter. Soon she saw the waitress and the cook whispering to each other. The waitress's red ponytail bobbed as she nodded.

Then the cook looked toward Nancy's booth. Within minutes the cook and the waitress returned. The cook was not a large man, but his eyes were a piercing steel gray.

"I'm afraid you'll have to leave," the cook said to Nancy. The waitress looked a little frightened as she stood next to the booth.

"Excuse me?" Nancy said. It was a question, not a statement.

"I want you out of here," the cook said. "Now." He turned to the waitress. "Clear this table," he ordered.

With an apologetic half-smile, the waitress began taking water glasses and napkins away from Nancy, Bess, George, and Ned.

"Wait a minute," Ned said. "What's going on here? We ordered some sodas."

"The diner's closed," the owner said. "Especially to you four. Now I want you to get up and leave."

"But the sign says you're open," Nancy said without moving.

"Not to you," the cook said. "Not to friends of Katie Firestone. This is a private party."

Bess, Ned, and George looked at Nancy for direction. She was suddenly aware that Joan Kim had stopped talking.

"Hey, it's those outsiders that was askin' questions last night," one of the fishermen yelled from across the diner. Nancy recognized him from their meeting on the pier.

"They got no business being here," a woman shouted. "Get 'em out."

Several people came over to Nancy's booth as if to back up the cook. Nancy stood, saying, "We're not here to make trouble. We stopped in for sodas, that's all."

Ned, Bess, and George slid out of the booth and followed Nancy to the door. Nancy could feel the waves of anger and fear that filled the room. She knew they had to leave.

"Whew," Bess said, climbing onto Katie's red bike. "I'm glad we're out here in the fresh air—even if it is foggy. That place is really creepy." They looked back to see the cook's face glowering at them from the window of the diner.

"And how about that Joan Kim," George said. "Did you hear her say nothing fatal or strictly illegal? Wow! It gave me chills."

"Who is this Joan Kim?" Ned asked. "And where's she from?"

"I don't know," Nancy said, maneuvering her bike onto the road. "But I'm going to find out!"

There was no traffic on the two-lane road down the coast to Katie's and the inn where Nancy, Ned, and Bess were staying. The four took turns leading, then falling back. After about two miles, George took the lead, followed by Ned, then Bess.

Nancy was last and lost in thought. It was no coincidence that Joan Kim showed up at the Seabreak diner, she concluded. I'm sure someone invited her there. Was it Holt Scotto? And where was he anyway? I would have thought he'd be front and center for that meeting.

Nancy's thoughts were interrupted by Bess's voice from the road ahead. "I'll take the lead now," she said.

Nancy watched her ride to the front as George fell back to second place.

Nancy returned to her thoughts, turning the events of the last two days over and over in her mind.

So Joan Kim outfoxed Andy Jason, Nancy thought. That wasn't easy, I'll bet. He's pretty smooth. I wonder how she did it. Maybe I should contact Jason to talk to him about it.

Bess led them up a small rise in the road. There were still no cars in either direction. The wind was chilly and the wisps of fog were getting thicker.

Who invited Joan Kim to Seabreak, Nancy wondered. Was it Holt Scotto?

"Whoa," Bess called, interrupting Nancy's thoughts. "Hey, there's something wrong with my bike. It's wobbling, and—"

A nasty snap of metal cut off Bess's words. Then her cry pierced the fog. Bess's bike seemed to fly apart.

Horrified, Nancy watched Bess barrel into Ned, somersaulting over his back wheel and landing with a horrible scraping skid on the side of the road.

Bess landed in the dirt. She didn't move or cry out.

Ned couldn't keep his balance and tumbled sideways, smashing his bike into a small fir tree.

7

Strike Two

Nancy skidded to a stop and ran to Bess, who lay on the ground, her arm twisted beneath her handlebars. Her right calf was scraped raw and bleeding, but she was conscious.

"Bess, how do you feel?" Nancy asked. She unbuttoned Bess's jacket and then checked her pulse. "Do you feel dizzy? Or sick to your stomach? Did you hit your head?"

"My wrist hurts," Bess answered, "but I think I'm okay otherwise." Carefully, Nancy and George lifted the handlebars off Bess's arm. The front wheel of her bike lay about four yards down the road.

Ned struggled to his feet and shook his head and

arms. "Are you okay, Ned?" Nancy called back over her shoulder.

"Yeah, I'm fine," Ned said. He walked over to where Nancy kneeled cautiously feeling Bess's wrist.

"I don't think it's broken," Nancy said. "But we need to have a doctor check it out, just in case. I don't like the looks of that scrape on your leg either, Bess."

"What scrape?" Bess leaned up a little on one elbow and looked at her left leg. Blood trickled down from a bad scrape the size of her hand. Bits of dirt and weeds clung to her raw flesh. "Wow," Bess said. "I can't even feel that. But it looks horrible."

"You're in shock," Nancy pointed out. "You hit pretty hard."

"You're going to feel it later, I'll bet," George said. "What happened?"

"I don't know exactly," Bess said. "My front wheel started to sort of shimmy, and then I hit that bump, and . . . I don't know . . . it just seemed to fly apart."

"We passed a pay phone," George said. "I'll ride back and call Katie. She can pick Bess up and take her to a doctor or a clinic somewhere. I don't think they've got one in Seabreak."

George rode off, and Nancy and Ned did what they could to make Bess comfortable. Ned eased his folded jacket under her head. Nancy carefully dabbed at Bess's wound with a tissue.

"Are you sure you're okay, Ned?" Nancy asked. "You hit that tree pretty hard."

"I'm okay. Actually, the bike took most of the impact. Looks like Katie has some major bike rehab work ahead of her."

"Especially on the one Bess was riding," Nancy said. She and Ned gathered up the parts of Bess's bike and put them in a pile.

Ned studied Bess's broken bike.

"You know a lot about bikes, Ned. Can you tell what happened?" Nancy asked.

"It looks like one of the cone nuts might have come loose," Ned told her. "This is a cone nut and the washer that goes with it." He opened his hand and showed her. "I found them near the bump in the road, near where Bess said the bike broke apart."

Ned picked up the front of the bike, which was no longer connected to the wheel. "This two-pronged metal piece that runs down from the handlebars is called the fork," he said. "It holds the wheel on. The axle runs between the two prongs of the fork and is held on by the cone nuts on both sides."

He pointed to the nut and washer on the left side. "See, here are the cone nut and washer on this side. They're still intact." Then he pointed to the right side of the fork. "But this side of the axle isn't connected to the fork anymore. It pulled away, the wheel spun off, and Bess was dumped."

"And the axle pulled apart because the nut came off?" Nancy repeated.

"Right," Ned said. "It must have been loose."

George came shooting back on her bike. "Katie's on her way. She says the nearest clinic is about thirty miles down the coast. She called their twenty-four-hour emergency number to tell them we're coming."

"That sounds like where we were this morning," Bess said, "around where Andy Jason's office is."

Katie arrived just a few minutes later. Ned and Nancy helped Bess into the second seat of Katie's van, where she could stretch out.

Katie and George fastened the bikes that Nancy and George had ridden on to the racks on top of the van. Nancy and Ned took the seats at the back of the van just in front of the hold where Katie had thrown the damaged bikes. George and Katie jumped into the front seat, and they headed down the coast.

During the ride to the clinic, Nancy and her friends told Katie about the possible stalker in the Cypress Cathedral and the confrontation in the diner.

At the clinic, Bess had a wrist X ray. Ned was also checked over and pronounced healthy.

Katie and George stayed with Bess while her leg was being cleaned and bandaged.

After Ned was released, Nancy got the keys to Katie's van, then she and Ned went outside. "I want to take another look at that bike axle," Nancy said, unlocking the back of the van.

Ned took out the broken bike that had thrown Bess. They both checked it over carefully in the light from the interior of the van. Finally Ned spoke. "Do you think the cone nut could have been loosened on purpose?" he wondered, his voice hushed.

"Well, it just seems odd that it would be loose," Nancy said. "Katie rehabs these bikes and keeps them in shape herself. She seems to be very thorough. I can't see her climbing on a bike without checking to make sure the cone nuts are secure and everything's in good shape. It just doesn't make sense."

Nancy aimed her penlight at the end of the axle that had disconnected. She bent down to get a closer look. "There!" she said. "Look at that!"

Ned bent over and squinted into the thin beam of bright light. "Whoa," he said in a whisper.

"It's been cut," Nancy said quietly, running her finger around the end of the axle. "Someone cut it about halfway through," she added, as she felt the smooth edge around part of the rim. Then her finger hit a sharp jagged point.

"When she hit the bump . . ." Ned began.

"It snapped the rest of the way," Nancy finished.

"Well, if it isn't Miss Lowell." A familiar voice spoke from behind her. Startled, Nancy felt her shoulders jump. Then she turned to see Andy Jason walking toward her.

Nancy turned back to close the van. "I'm Linnie Lowell," she whispered to Ned. Then she turned back to face the approaching Jason.

"Mr. Jason," she said, extending her hand.

"Andy, remember?" Jason said, giving her a firm handshake and gesturing with the other hand toward the clinic door. "What are you doing here? Not ill, I hope."

"No, my friend—actually, my photographer, Jane. You remember her, I'm sure. She took a spill off her bike and we brought her here for an X ray. This is Ned N . . . Nordstrom," she added, nodding at Ned.

"Nice to meet you." Jason shook Ned's hand. Ned smiled and then mumbled a greeting.

"I was at the library," Jason said, pointing to a small building across the road. "We've just had a little presentation there about whales and their migrating habits. Sorry you didn't know about it. You might have enjoyed my talk."

"I'm sure I would have," Nancy said, smiling. "Well, Jane is probably ready now. It was nice seeing you again." She turned to go back to the clinic.

"Miss Lowell?" Jason called to her. "What's this? Riding with the competition?"

Nancy turned to see Jason reading the sign painted on the side of Katie's van.

"Actually, Ms. Firestone drove by as Jane fell and kindly offered us a ride to the clinic." Nancy was diving deeper into deception with every word. She knew she needed to get into the clinic to warn the others before they came out and blew her cover.

"Really," Jason said. He gave her a quizzical look, and for a moment she was sure he didn't believe her. But why wouldn't he, she asked herself. He has no reason to suspect me.

"It was nice to see you again, Mr. Jason," Nancy said. "Now, if you'll excuse us, we should go in."

"Yes, well, of course," Jason said. He started to back up, watching Nancy carefully. "You tell that Katie Firestone that I never give up," he called out. "She hasn't heard the last from me."

Nancy smiled and waved. Then she and Ned raced up the clinic steps and into the building. The doctor was telling Bess that a radiologist would call about the X ray results the next day.

While they all walked to the van, Nancy and Ned told the others about their meeting with Andy Jason.

As Katie backed the van out of the clinic parking lot, Nancy noticed a large luxury car parked in the shadows, away from the lights.

Katie pulled out onto the road. From her vantage point at the window in the rear of the van, Nancy saw the face of the driver in the luxury car. It was Andy Jason, and he was definitely watching them.

"Katie, I need to stop at the sheriff's office on the way back," Nancy said. "I want to show him your bike."

"What are you saying?" Bess asked, sitting up with a start. "Are you telling me that it wasn't an accident?"

Nancy and Ned told the others their suspicions. "When she hit that bump, the axle broke," Nancy concluded.

"Boy, Jenna's going to be sorry she hit the sack early," Katie muttered. "She missed all the excitement."

No one spoke again until they reached the sheriff's office. Nancy, Ned, and Katie took the bike into the small building. Sheriff Harvey was just leaving, so they gave him a quick report and left the broken bike.

The sheriff seemed very interested in Nancy and Ned's theory of the bike accident. He also told them he expected to have analysis of the fingerprints taken from Katie's vandalized boat by the next day. Nancy also mentioned the possible stalking incident in the Cypress Cathedral.

When they reached the inn where Nancy, Ned, and Bess were staying, Katie and George dropped them off. "I think you all need to sleep in a little tomorrow," Katie said. "Why don't you come down to the house about ten. We'll have a late breakfast." Nancy and Ned waved the others off, then helped Bess limp into the inn.

Upstairs, Ned went on to his room, and Nancy unlocked the door to the room she shared with Bess.

Bess complained that her leg was starting to get pretty sore. She limped and hopped into the room and over to her bed. As she made her way, she dragged a small piece of folded paper halfway across the rag rug. Finally Bess's foot left the paper behind as she climbed up on her bed.

Nancy reached down to pick up the piece of paper. Clutching the note, she turned her back to Bess and unfolded the paper to find a handprinted note.

So sorry your friend got hurt, but it's your fault. This is just the beginning unless you back off and stay out of things that are none of your business.

8

Surf's Up!

"Ooooooh," Bess moaned. "My leg really hurts."

"Um . . . yes, the doctor gave you some medicine for the pain," Nancy said, quickly slipping the note into a jeans pocket. "I'll get you something to drink."

Nancy took a bottle of juice from the minibar. In the bathroom decorated with blue and gold tiles, she poured the juice into a glass.

I'm not going to tell Bess about the note tonight, she thought. Tomorrow's soon enough. Bess is already upset and sore, and what she really needs is a good night's sleep.

Nancy took the note from her pocket and read it again. Holt Scotto knows where our room is, she thought. *He was here last night.* She slipped the note back in her pocket, her mind awhirl. *Scotto's car was parked outside the diner earlier,* she told herself, *and he wasn't inside. He could have cut the axle then. But what about Andy Jason? Why was he hanging around the clinic after we talked? He was definitely watching us. Why?*

"Proof," she mumbled as she stopped at the mini-bar again to get a couple of ice cubes. "I need clues."

"Hmmm?" Bess said wearily from her bed. "What'd you say?"

"We need a break in this case," Nancy said.

"Oooooh, don't say the word *break* to someone who's just crashed a bicycle," Bess groaned with a lopsided smile.

"Right," Nancy said, grinning. "Do you need anything?"

"Ten hours of sleep," Bess said, taking her medicine and finishing her juice before falling heavily back on the bed.

"I'm going to run down to the reception area," Nancy said. "Back in a minute."

"Mm-hmm," Bess hummed, her eyes closed.

Nancy went downstairs, where she found Mrs. Oprey, the innkeeper.

"Good evening," Nancy said. She took a deep breath and gave the woman a warm smile. She didn't want to alarm Mrs. Oprey or even make her suspicious. "Did anyone stop by to see Bess, Ned, or me this evening?"

"Why, no," Mrs. Oprey said. "Were you expecting someone?"

"Well, yes, actually. I didn't know whether they'd stop by or not. We hadn't heard from them."

"Who were you expecting?"

"Friends of ours from River Heights," Nancy said. "A man and a woman. Or maybe just one of them. They weren't sure they could both make it. We thought we'd be home sooner than we were."

"Well, I wasn't down here every minute, of course, but I don't believe anyone came."

"Thanks," Nancy said. "I'm sure we'll hear from them tomorrow." She smiled again and went back upstairs. Her bed and the soft quilts were a welcome haven.

Nancy awoke early Wednesday morning and went onto the tiny balcony outside her room. The air was damp and foggy.

Nancy read the note again. It was in pencil, hand-printed in block capital letters. Apparently, the author knew that would make it more difficult to identify the handwriting. Someone sneaked up here and slipped this note under our door, Nancy told herself. Someone who knew our room number.

She went inside. Bess was still sleeping soundly. Nancy sat at the desk in the corner of the room and dialed the sheriff's office.

"Hello, Sheriff Harvey," she said, keeping her voice low so she wouldn't wake Bess. "Did you get the fingerprint report yet?"

"Yes, I did," the sheriff told her. "The fingerprints we lifted from Katie Firestone's boat do *not* match anything we have on file here."

"Have you heard of anyone named Joan Kim?" Nancy asked. She told the sheriff about the meeting in the diner the night before.

"Just what I need," he grumbled. "Another outsider poking around. I don't mean you, of course, Ms. Drew," he said quickly. "You're practically a professional, from what Katie says. Well, I guess I'd better find out who Joan Kim is and what she's doing around here."

Then Nancy told Sheriff Harvey about the threatening note she had received.

"It seems my work is cut out for me today, isn't it?" the sheriff replied. "I don't like the sound of that note one bit. I'll send someone over to pick it up right away."

"I'll leave it at the desk with Mrs. Oprey," Nancy told him.

When she hung up, she copied the message in her notebook. Then she put the original in an envelope, sealed it, put the sheriff's name on the front, and ran it down to the large antique desk Mrs. Oprey used for guest check-in.

By the time Nancy returned to the room, Bess was up and getting dressed. "How are you feeling?" Nancy asked, watching Bess pull wide-leg blue cotton pants gingerly up over her scraped leg.

"Like I've been hit by a sneaker wave," Bess answered, moaning. "Actually, it doesn't hurt as much as I thought it would. I'm not going to be doing any kayaking today, though."

"I'm not sure anyone is," Nancy said, gazing out the window. "It's pretty foggy out there."

They finished getting ready about the time Ned rapped on their door. He helped Bess down the stairs, and Nancy drove their rental car to Katie's.

Over breakfast Nancy told the others about the note and showed them the copy she had made. "Katie and George told me about your adventures out on the bluffs and at the diner," Jenna said. "And I was so sorry to hear about Bess's crash. How are you doing this morning, Bess?"

"Better, thanks," Bess said, smearing a muffin with boysenberry jam.

Nancy told everyone about her conversation with Sheriff Harvey.

"I think he was trying to tell us something when he emphasized that he didn't have anything on file that matched the prints," Katie said. "Holt Scotto got in some trouble a few months ago. There was

71

some kind of brawl outside the diner, and he and some others were taken in by the sheriff. They were booked and spent the night in jail, I think, but they were released the next day."

"So he would have Scotto's prints on file," Ned concluded.

"Which still doesn't rule him out," George pointed out, peeling an orange. "Even though his prints don't match the ones Sheriff Harvey collected, it doesn't mean he didn't do it. He could have worn gloves, for example."

"Did the sheriff say he was going to talk to this Scotto person about any of this?" Jenna asked.

"Not exactly," Nancy said. "He didn't like the looks of the axle on the bicycle, though, and he sent someone over right away to pick up the note."

"Sheriff Harvey is a good man," Katie said. "I trust him to do everything he can."

"I don't see how anyone can track down who wrote that note," Jenna said. "Not if it looked the way you said, and the innkeeper didn't see who delivered it."

"What I can't figure out," Nancy said, her eyes narrowing as she thought, "is how someone knew about Bess's accident so soon after it happened. Unless, of course, that person was following us."

Everyone was quiet for a moment, lost in their own thoughts.

"It's like you said, Nancy," Katie finally noted.

"This is a small town. I'm always amazed at how fast news—and rumors—spread."

Katie, Jenna, and George were determined to go kayaking, so after breakfast they started packing up the gear. Jenna had brought a spare kayak but seemed reluctant to lend it. Katie had three spares, and since Bess would be staying on shore, Nancy, Ned, and George were all supplied.

"This is a great spot for sea kayaking," Katie said. "It has the perfect balance of wind, waves, and tide. And it's kind of remote, so we shouldn't be bothered by anyone."

"Good," Bess said. "I want the beach to myself."

They decided to take both Katie's and Jenna's vans, and by noon, they had both vehicles packed. As they were walking to the car, the phone rang. Katie went in to answer it, in case it was the sheriff with news about his investigation.

As the others milled around the vans, Andy Jason's large luxury car glided into Katie's driveway.

Nancy was instantly on guard, remembering the way he had watched them pulling out of the clinic parking lot the night before.

"Well, Jane," Andy Jason said to Bess as he climbed out of the car. "I hope you're better this morning?" He looked down at her wrist, wrapped in an elastic bandage.

"Hello, Linnie," Andy said, turning to Nancy. "So I find you with Katie Firestone again."

Over Jason's shoulder, Nancy could see Jenna. The young woman looked surprised when she heard Andy call Nancy and Bess by their undercover names. Then Nancy saw George and Ned take Jenna's arms and pull her behind the van. Nancy was sure they were filling her in.

"Hello, Andy," Katie said, as she walked out of the house and down the driveway. "How come every time I turn around, you're there?"

"I'm just here to lend a hand," Andy said in a jovial, good-natured manner. "I heard your boat was trashed, and I'm here to offer you one of mine to use till yours gets fixed."

"I appreciate it, but you wasted a trip," Katie answered. "My boat is back in working order."

"It's interesting that you should bring up the vandalizing of Ms. Firestone's boat," Nancy said, thinking fast. "As a matter of fact, that's why Janie and I are here. She told us about it when she kindly gave us a ride last night. We came back this morning to get a story about the incident for the *Canyon Courier.*" She smiled at Andy.

"How did you find out about it?" Nancy asked. "I'm surprised word got down the coast so fast. Were you in our area when it happened, by any chance?"

For a moment Andy glared at Nancy, searching her expression. Then he relaxed and said with a grin, "Why, we whale watchers have to stick together, right, Katie?" He turned away from Nancy toward Katie. "You know, if you'd just work for me, you wouldn't have these kinds of problems."

"What's that supposed to mean?" Katie asked.

"I just meant that if your boat was part of my fleet, you'd get the advantage of my full security force and system behind you. Your boat wouldn't have to sit isolated on some dock where anyone could come aboard, ransack it, and tear up your motor."

"Andy, give it up," Katie said. "I'm staying independent—you might as well accept it."

"Okay, okay, I'll leave, but I'm not giving up," he said, shaking his head as he walked back to his car. "You *will* come to work for me." He gave them all a jaunty wave and drove off.

"I tell you, that guy gives me the creeps," George said as she, Ned, and Jenna emerged from behind the van. "He's just too smooth."

"It was the clinic that called," Katie reported. "Bess, your wrist is definitely not broken, but it is sprained. You need to keep it wrapped for a few days and not use it too much."

"Sounds like an afternoon of lazy beachcombing is an approved activity," Bess said, heading for Katie's van. "Let's get going."

"I agree," Jenna said. "It's time to forget all this detective stuff and get on with our real mission in life—sea kayaking!" She checked all her gear one last time. "Wait a minute," she said. "Where's my helmet? Did someone take my helmet?"

Everyone checked the helmets in both vans. Jenna's was definitely missing. "I have a couple of extras packed," Katie said. "You can use one of them. Come on, we need to go. It's nearly an hour's drive, and there's a killer fog that rolls in up there. If we get stuck in it, it could be dangerous."

They all piled in the vans and took off. Nancy and Ned rode with Jenna, Bess and George with Katie. Each van had two kayaks fastened on the top and one resting in the back. Piles of wet suits, paddles, helmets, goggles, and other gear took up the rest of the space.

They finally came to a desolate stretch of coastline that seemed to go on for miles. There were no buildings, not even a cabin or motel.

"This must be private property," Nancy reasoned. "There's no development anywhere." Within minutes, they came to a high wire fence with simple No Trespassing signs posted on it.

Katie led Jenna down a road that ran along the outside of the fence to the shore. They parked the vans and began unloading their gear. Jenna changed to her wet suit and grabbed her kayak and gear. Then she ran to the beach. Bess ambled slowly after her.

This area was different from the sea lion nursery beach. There were huge rock formations farther out in the water but few close to shore.

"George, I know you've kayaked in surf," Katie

said, "but, Nancy and Ned, you need a quick course on how to maneuver in this water. Let's get the gear out, and I'll give you some pointers."

They changed into their wet suits, and then unpacked the vans and spread the gear out. "First, everybody gets an emergency kit," Katie said, passing out the items. "Keep two pocket flares inside your wet suit and two larger parachute flares on the boat. If you're in trouble, fire a large one first. It can be seen as far as ten or fifteen miles and goes up about fifteen hundred feet. The pocket flares attract someone closer and go up a third as far."

Out of the corner of her eye, Nancy saw Jenna standing at the edge of the water trying on one of Katie's helmets. Bess sat at the back of the beach on a large piece of driftwood next to Jenna's kayak, sifting the sand through her fingers.

As Nancy pulled on her lifejacket, the sound of Bess yelling caused her to look up immediately. Bess had gotten up and was limping toward the water. Her arm was outstretched as if she were reaching for something.

Nancy started toward Bess—walking at first, then breaking into a run. She could hear George, Katie, and Ned following her.

Nancy kept her eyes on Bess, limping slowly toward the water. It was almost like watching a movie in slow motion. Bess seemed to be yelling again, but Nancy couldn't hear her over the low roar of the surf.

As Nancy sprinted across the beach, she looked in the direction Bess was reaching. In horror, she saw what Bess was yelling about.

A huge wave was roaring toward the shore. Unaware, Jenna, her back to the ocean, was adjusting the helmet around her ears.

Nancy ran faster, but she was too late. No one could reach Jenna in time. Helpless, Nancy watched the wave fold over the beach and crash. When the foam and water retreated, Jenna was gone.

9

From C to C

Nancy, George, Ned, and Katie went back for their kayaks and paddles and raced toward the water. "It was a sneaker!" Katie yelled. "We've got to get out of here!"

As she pulled on her helmet, Nancy stared at the azure blue sea, straining to see Jenna. She zipped the pocket flares into her wet suit and tucked the parachute flares in the forward bulkhead, as Katie had shown her.

Then she put her kayak in the shallow water. Bracing herself with her paddle, she stepped into the boat. Sliding her feet forward to the foot braces, she lowered herself into the seat of the cockpit.

Within minutes she felt the tide lift her and carry her quickly away from shore.

Nancy and the others paddled out about fifty yards, looking for Jenna and calling her name. There were no rocks breaking the surface in this immediate area, but Nancy knew some were hidden under the water.

If Jenna hit one of those rocks, Nancy thought, she could be unconscious . . . or worse. We've got to reach her—fast.

She stroked her paddle through the water, watching for any sign. Finally she saw something. It was Jenna's helmet, breaking the surface of the wave. Then her head came up, and Nancy saw her lie back on the water's surface, gulping air.

"There she is," Nancy yelled to the others. She pointed with her paddle toward Jenna, bobbing in the surf as she skimmed over the waves about ten yards away.

The four rescuers paddled rapidly toward Jenna. Katie and George reached her first. Nancy struggled as she paddled against the current, but she and Ned finally arrived.

"How is she?" Nancy called out. "Is she all right?"

"She's fine," Katie said, giving the thumbs-up sign.

Nancy turned toward shore and gave Bess a wave with her paddle. She could hear Bess's cheer float across the water.

"Thanks for coming out so quickly, everybody,"

Jenna said between coughs. She lay back on the surface, her lifejacket keeping her afloat.

"You're sure you're okay?" Nancy asked.

Jenna nodded and smiled.

"Jenna is a real pro," Katie said. "This may have been her first time with a sneaker wave, but it sure isn't the first time she's been dumped in the surf."

"Yeah, but usually my kayak is somewhere nearby," Jenna called back, spitting a mouthful of salt water over her shoulder. She pulled up a little on the bow of Katie's kayak, resting her elbows on the deck. "So what's a sneaker wave anyway, and how come you didn't warn me about them?"

"Sorry," Katie said, with an apologetic smile. "I told the others, but I guess I forgot to tell you."

"I've had quite a few surf spills in my career, but this was one of the worst," Jenna said, glowering at Katie. "And you're going to pay for it, too," she added, "with the hardest workout you've ever had. To start with, you can pull me back to shore to get my kayak."

Katie groaned, in mock distress. Jenna floated around to the stern of Katie's kayak and grasped the grab loop firmly, her legs bobbing up behind her. "Okay, Firestone," she ordered. "Start paddling."

When Katie and Jenna started for shore, George took over as the most experienced sea kayaker and instructor. "Let's go in a little closer to shore," she said to Nancy and Ned. "I want you to practice some moves, and I'd feel more comfortable if we were in shallower water."

The three paddled in a little, then George stopped and turned to Nancy and Ned. It looked as if they were about the length of a football field out from the shore.

"You've both kayaked," George said, "so I'm not going to go over the paddle strokes. Just ask if you have any questions."

For the next half hour George demonstrated how to read the waves and work with the currents. She also gave them a quick refresher course on how to recover from a roll or a capsize. They practiced both the "C to C" and "lie-back" methods of recovery.

By the time George had finished their mini training session, Nancy could see that Bess was combing the beach once again.

Jenna had gotten her kayak, and she and Katie were back out in the water. In fact, they were already at least fifty yards farther out than Nancy, George, and Ned.

Nancy could see by George's expression that she wanted to be out with Katie and Jenna getting in a real workout.

"Go on out, George," Nancy said. "Ned and I will be okay."

"Are you sure?" George asked.

"Hey, we're not total amateurs, you know," Ned

said, twirling his kayak around a couple of times. "Don't worry—we'll watch out for each other."

"Great," George said with a grin. "I really want to get some serious training in, and it looks like that fog is starting to move in already." With a wave of her paddle, George headed out toward Katie and Jenna.

Nancy and Ned paddled around for a while. Working with the surf was very different from working with river currents. It was also very exciting and a lot of fun.

Nancy and Ned challenged each other to a few manuevers, and the time flew by. Nancy figured an hour had passed, at least, and it must have been close to four o'clock.

The sun was low, and the fog bank was floating very slowly across the sea toward them. She could barely see Katie, George, and Jenna bobbing in the orangey blue waves.

Nancy idled awhile, enjoying floating with the tide. She watched Ned tilt and dunk and practice his rolls. Finally he surfaced near her. "Hey, Nan," he called, "how about a race? I'll give you a two-minute head start."

"You're on," Nancy said, "and you'll be sorry you gave me any time at all."

Nancy dug her paddle into the water and headed out on a line parallel to the shore. They were a little farther out than they had been, but the sea was pretty calm.

She looked back to try to see Bess, but Nancy and

Ned had worked their way farther north. Large rock formations, which had once seemed far away, were close now. The rock formations towered up out of the sea, blocking her view. She wasn't really able to see Bess's beach anymore.

Suddenly Nancy felt herself being pulled out to the left by a strong current. She paddled against it for a while, but she felt the pull getting stronger as she got more tired.

She looked around for a minute to signal Ned but couldn't see him through the wispy fog that had begun to envelop the area. When she looked forward again, she realized she'd been pulled rapidly out in just that minute she'd taken to look for Ned.

I know I'm being pulled farther out, she thought, because those rocks are getting closer.

One of the rocks was huge—the size of a small building. When the light reflected at just the right angle off the water, she thought she saw a dark opening in the side of the rock.

She looked back toward the shore and could barely make out Ned in the distance. He was paddling rapidly toward her, but seemed to be falling farther and farther back.

"He's not going backward," she mumbled, as she realized what was happening. "I'm moving forward—and way too fast."

The current really seemed to have a hold of her now. It was almost as if her kayak had a motor. Even the tide had no effect on it. She felt as if she had no control over her craft.

Suddenly the kayak listed sharply to the left. Holding tightly to her paddle, Nancy followed Katie's and George's instructions and rolled with the kayak.

She used the "C to C" recovery maneuver, making her body into a C in one direction as she rolled under the water, then forming a C in the opposite direction to pull herself back up out of the water.

In seconds she was upright again. She blew out a mouthful of spicy salt water and gulped in air. It seemed to have become suddenly dark, so she lifted her goggles to get a better view. She stopped cold when she realized why it was dark.

The sun and sky were completely blocked out by the enormous bulk of the huge rock tower. She was headed right toward the opening in the side. Her arms flailed against the waves, but her effort was useless. With one giant surge, Nancy and her kayak were flung through the opening into a dark sea cave.

10

Here's Looking at You

Nancy's heartbeat surged with the wave that carried her into the sea cave. Suddenly her kayak slowed, and she drifted for a few minutes before hitting the inner wall of the cave. As the kayak floated, she felt her racing pulse slow, and she took a deep breath.

She looked around as her eyes adjusted to the dim light. It was like being in a cave on land, except the floor of the cave was the sea.

The cave had been dug into the huge rock tower that rose up from the ocean floor and arched high over the water's surface. Over centuries the sea had hollowed out the rock into a long dark grotto.

A few columns of light filtered down through holes in the high ceiling of the cave. Nancy's kayak was tangled in webs of kelp that had been swept into the cave with her. The water inside the cave was calm and dark, but it was periodically flushed by a wave of foam.

Nancy's kayak bumped against a ledge that protruded from the cave wall. She could see that in some places the ledge was under water and in some places it skimmed the surface. In front of her, the ledge formed a platform that jutted out several yards above the water's surface.

Nancy placed her paddle on the ledge. Then she hoisted herself out of the cockpit and onto the ledge, pulling her kayak up next to her.

She tried to stand up, but her legs were so wobbly, she had to drop down to a crouch. Then she sat, pulling her knees up and leaning her back against the shiny damp wall of the cave.

Nancy rubbed her calves and knees. Then she leaned back again, took a deep breath, and rested for a few minutes.

"Nancy," Ned's familiar voice called out. "Nancy, are you in here? Where are you?"

"Over here, Ned," Nancy called back.

"See, I told you she'd be okay," George told Ned as they paddled toward Nancy's ledge.

"George!" Nancy said. "What are you doing here? The last time I saw you, you were way out with Katie and Jenna."

"Yeah, well, it wasn't much fun," George replied.

"They have a real competitive thing going on—I mean, they are ferocious. There's no way I could keep up, so I thought I'd come back and whip you beginners. As I was paddling in, I saw that surge take you into the cave. Ned and I got here about the same time."

"This is really cool," Ned said, paddling in a circle so he could check out the cave.

"Let's do a little exploring," Nancy said. "Do Katie and Jenna know where we are, George?"

"They don't know anything right now but how much they want to beat each other. They couldn't care less where—or how—we are." She checked her sports watch. "We've got at least another hour before they'll be ready to call it quits."

"Good!" Nancy said. George and Ned held her kayak steady while she climbed back into her cockpit. "Come on," she said, as she settled into her seat and braced her legs. "Let's take a look around."

Nancy led the others toward what she thought was the back of the cave. The paddling was so much easier in the calm water. The farther back they went into the large space, the quieter it got. Soon even the roar of the surf was like a distant echo.

Nancy was surprised to find there was more than one "room" in the cave. They wandered in and out of openings and archways for about half an hour. Occasionally, they realized they had gotten turned around and had backtracked into an area they had already explored. Finally they came to a small room that was almost bright compared to some of the others they had been in.

A large hole at the top of the cave released a thick shaft of light into the center of the small room. Even a few wisps of fog drifted down around them.

"I have to pull over to a ledge for a minute," Ned said. "I want to stretch my legs. I'm getting a cramp."

Nancy and George followed him over to the wall of the small room. Ned got out of his kayak and did a few quadriceps stretches. The light was dimmer at the edge, but something still caught Nancy's eye.

Something shiny glinted through the water from a section of the ledge that was just below the surface. She paddled over and reached under the water. The object seemed to shimmer as the water moved over it. She took hold of it, but it was jammed into a crack in the inner wall of the cave.

Patiently she tugged at the object, jiggling it until she finally pulled it free. "Hey, look at this," she called to George and Ned.

It was a silver belt buckle in the shape of a horse's head with a windswept mane.

"Very cool," George said. "It looks almost new."

"I know," Nancy agreed. "It can't have been in here for long. The salt hasn't affected it much yet. The only real marks are where it was wedged into the rock."

"I wonder how it got in here," Ned said.

"The same way I did, probably," Nancy said. "It

had no choice." She zipped the buckle into her wet suit.

Nancy and George held Ned's kayak as he climbed back into the cockpit. "How are your legs?" she asked him.

"Better," he said. "The stretches really helped."

"Ready to do some more exploring?" Nancy asked Ned and George.

"Lead the way," George replied.

As Nancy paddled away from the ledge, she heard an odd sound. It was almost like a whisper echoing around the walls of the cave.

"Did you hear that?" she asked, her voice hushed as she listened.

"What? I didn't hear anything," Ned said. He sounded a little impatient. "You know what? I'm ready to get out of here. I feel like we've been going in circles. I'm ready for some daylight. Maybe we should hook back up with Katie and Jenna."

"Shhh," Nancy said, idling her kayak. She closed her eyes, hoping that would help her concentrate on hearing.

As she drifted, she heard the sound again. A low whisper floated through the fog. She couldn't make out any words exactly. It was more like a low whooshing moan from behind her. The sound floated over her like the filmy fog. It was strange and eerie. A shiver cascaded down her spine as she looked around.

"There," she said, her eyes popping open again. "Did you hear that?" She looked eagerly at her friends.

"I hear a sort of distant roaring noise," George said. "I'm sure it's the waves breaking in the distance," George said. "Is that what you mean?" She leaned her head out as if she were reaching for the sound.

"I'm not hearing anything but my stomach growling," Ned said. "I'm getting out of this place."

"Go ahead if you want," Nancy said. "I'm not leaving until I check out that noise." She pointed her kayak in the direction of the sound. She paddled through an arch to a dim circle of light in the far wall.

"I don't think we've been in here yet," George said.

"Well, that's a first," Ned answered. "We've backtracked so much, I thought we'd made a complete tour of this cave at least twice."

"I guess I was wrong," George said. "Looks like we're back at the front of the cave again—or are we?" George asked. "That sure looks like an opening."

"It is, but I don't think it's the front," Nancy said. "I think that's the back of the cave. Come on, let's go."

She paddled off and reached the light within minutes. "See," Nancy called back to the others. "I knew it. It's like the back door of the cave."

She paddled through the small opening just as the deep whisper sounded again. Only this time, it was louder, nearer.

Nancy blinked for a minute when she emerged

from inside the rock. They were completely enclosed in a thick fog bank, but it was still much brighter than it had been in the dim regions within the cave. There was a pale pinkish glow off to their left, and Nancy assumed that was the sun setting in the west. She knew that meant the shore was to their right, but she couldn't see it through the fog.

She looked around. They had drifted forward far enough that she could barely see the outline of the sea cave behind them. She had never been in fog this thick and heavy.

Suddenly Nancy's kayak bumped into something hard. That eerie whisper curled toward her ears from the fog ahead of her. It was followed by a deep moan and then the whisper again.

"Nancy," George gasped, her voice low and a little shaky. "I hear it."

"Me, too," Ned whispered.

The three idled against the unyielding barrier they had bumped against. Nancy felt transfixed, hypnotized by the unearthly sound.

The soft whisper came closer and closer. Then something large and dark slowly broke the surface, and one huge eye stared straight at her.

11

Photographic Evidence

Nancy held her breath as she stared back at the large eye. No one made a sound. For a moment the fog broke and she could see the source of the sad-sounding whispers and moans.

A small whale stared right at her from some sort of holding pool.

"A whale," Ned said, his voice low. "It's a whale."

"A calf, I think," Nancy said. As she spoke, the whale disappeared beneath the surface. Nancy paddled along the perimeter of the pool, followed by Ned and George. But the barrier seemed endless.

"We'd better get back," George warned. "Katie'll have the Coast Guard out after us."

"I hate to leave, though," Nancy said. "I'm curious about what this pool is exactly. It's against the law for private citizens to capture whales, so this must be some scientific project. But I just want to make sure. I'd love to get another look at that calf."

"I agree with George. I'm tired and hungry. It's time to give it up for now, Nancy," Ned said.

Nancy knew they were right. She didn't want to worry the others. But she made a promise to herself to find out more about the whale calf and why it was trapped in the holding pool.

Nancy, Ned, and George started in the general direction of the shore. The fog made the trip confusing, and Nancy felt disoriented. Finally they reached some sea stacks near the shore.

"I don't remember these rocks when we first went out in our kayaks," George called out. "We were a little distracted by the sneaker, of course, but still . . ." She skillfully maneuvered her way around the stacks.

"This part of the shore doesn't look familiar at all," Ned said. "Where are we? It's hard to tell in this fog."

"We're a lot farther north than we were when Jenna was swept out," Nancy said, looking toward shore. "Let's go in here anyway. I'm ready to get out of this thing for a while."

"Even I'm ready," George said.

They half paddled, half drifted up to the shore.

When their kayaks bumped into the beach, they climbed out of the cockpits and stepped onto the sand.

"That's what I thought," Nancy said. "Look." She pointed to the bluffs in front of them. "We're north of where we started. This is that private property. Remember that fence we drove along to get down to the beach? I say we get out of here as fast as we can."

Nancy looked out across the ocean. She saw nothing but fog—no sea cave, no holding pool, no whale calf.

They drained the water from their kayaks. Then Nancy led Ned and George down the beach as fast as she could. It was a cumbersome hike. Their legs were still a little wobbly from being in the kayaks for so long. Balancing their kayaks and paddles on their shoulders also slowed them down.

Nancy kept pushing them faster. She couldn't shake the feeling that they needed to get off this property before the owner saw them, although she knew that was unlikely. By now they were completely enveloped by the fog bank as it headed for the forested hills.

They finally ran out of sandy beach and had to cross over large flat rocks, jumping from one to the other. At last they came to a metal staircase leading to the top of the bluff. They hoisted their kayaks up the steps and walked along the edge of the bluff until they came to the fence that ran along the side of the property.

Ned went over the fence first, then caught the kayaks and paddles as Nancy and George threw them over. The girls then scaled the fence and they were back on public property again.

Gratefully, they ran to the vans. Bess was waiting there, her jacket full of beautiful shells and large hunks of abalone. "Where have you been?" she cried when she saw Nancy. "We've been so worried!"

"You won't believe it," Nancy said, breathless from the fence climbing and the run. "Are Katie and Jenna back yet?"

"Been here and gone again," Bess said. "They're looking for you."

"They're not going to find much in this fog," Ned said. "I'll go on down to the beach and see if I can flag them in."

"Good," Nancy said. "We'll stay here in case you guys miss each other. Come back in fifteen minutes, no matter what, okay? If they're not back by then, we'll make a new plan. I don't want you guys to keep running back and forth missing each other."

"I want to warn you about something," Bess said. "Jenna is still mad at Katie."

"You mean because Katie forgot to warn her about sneaker waves?" George asked, slumping down to sit on the ground next to the van. "That's kind of lame. It was pretty scary, sure. But Jenna wasn't hurt. And Katie did apologize."

"Partly that, I think," Bess answered. "But I guess Katie really showed her up in their workout, too."

"Sort of adding insult to injury—literally," George said with a shrug.

"Exactly," Bess chimed in. "Anyway, Jenna's really burned. She's barely speaking."

"Well, sounds like she's had a pretty bad day so far," Ned said. "I can't really blame her if she's not in the best mood. Be back in fifteen or sooner."

Nancy, George, and Bess watched him walk a few yards before he disappeared into the fog.

While they waited, Nancy and George told Bess about the sea cave, the strange whispering sounds, and the whale calf.

"And I missed it," Bess said. "A baby whale right in front of you. Ohhhh, I wish I'd been there."

"It was truly cool," George said.

"You would have loved it, Bess," Nancy agreed. "But I still wonder what that whale is doing—"

Nancy's words were cut off by Ned's yells coming through the fog. "I found them," he called.

"*You* found *us?*" Katie said as they all joined Nancy, Bess, and George. "You three were the missing ones. We knew where we were the whole time, right, Jenna?"

"Yeah, right," Jenna muttered. "I'm changing my clothes." She packed up her kayak and gear, then got in her van and closed the door.

Nancy and the others took turns using Katie's van to change into jeans and sweaters. When everyone had changed and the gear was all packed, Nancy and Ned went back to Jenna's van.

Nancy almost felt as if she should knock, but when they got in, Jenna was her old self. "I'm hungry, aren't you," she said as Nancy and Ned climbed in the van. "Hope Katie's picked out a good place for dinner."

Jenna followed Katie back up the drive that ran along the high fence while Nancy and Ned told her about the whale calf. As they pulled out onto the coast road, Nancy took one last look back through the fence to the property beyond. I've got to find out who owns that land, she thought. And why they have a baby whale.

"So, Nancy, have you come up with any more ideas about who's been giving Katie so much trouble?" Jenna asked as she followed Katie's van down the coast highway.

The picture of the whale calf disappeared with a poof from Nancy's mind. Thoughts of Holt Scotto, Andy Jason, and Joan Kim rushed in. She realized that she hadn't given Katie's case a thought since Andy Jason had left the driveway that morning.

"No," Nancy said, focusing her thoughts. "No, I haven't."

After several miles of desolate, undeveloped coastline, they finally drove into a more populated area. Katie pulled her van into the parking lot of a pizza place.

Over dinner, the six talked about finding a whale calf in a holding pool.

"I just can hardly believe it," Katie said. "It is so against the law to tamper with these whales in any way. Are you sure it wasn't just a large porpoise or a shark or something? I mean, maybe after just coming out of that dark cave, and with the fog and everything . . ."

"It was definitely a whale," Nancy said.

"Maybe there was more than one," Bess wondered. "Do you suppose?"

"Actually, there could have been," George pointed out. "We only saw one end of the holding pool. It seemed to go on forever."

"Maybe that property belongs to some government agency or an environmental or scientific group of some kind," Jenna said. "Maybe they're doing research or rescuing orphan whales."

"I think I'd have heard about it, though," Katie said. "I mean it's pretty far away from where I live and everything, but I still think I would know about it. Especially since it's whales and all. I am sort of connected."

"Yeah, I suppose you're right," Jenna said.

"And besides, I read that even orphaned whales should be left alone if at all possible," Bess reported. "Other members of the group—"

"With whales, the group is called a pod," Katie interjected.

"Right," Bess continued. "Anyway, other members of the pod will usually adopt and rear them."

"And you didn't see any buildings on the property?" Jenna asked. "Nothing that could pass for a lab or an administration or office building?"

"No, but the fog was really thick," Ned pointed out.

"Nancy, you're so quiet," Bess observed. "You've hardly said a thing. What are you thinking?"

Nancy put down her piece of pizza and declared, "I'm going back up there tomorrow morning. Early—when the fog is far out over the ocean. Maybe then I can see what's really going on."

"Me, too," Bess said. "I'm going, too. I can't wait to see the baby whale."

"Sounds like fun," Ned said. "Sign me up."

"I'm going to pass," Katie said. "As much as I'd like to go, I've got to have another major workout. I've already lost too much time this week with all the harassment."

"Katie, we're going to solve this case," Nancy said. "I am going to find out who's been bothering you, I promise. I just need a few hours tomorrow morning to check out this whale thing."

"I believe you," Katie said, smiling warmly.

"I'm sticking with Katie tomorrow," Jenna said, with a mock frown. "I've got to get back at her for today."

"George, how about you?" Bess asked.

"Boy, I don't know. Both plans sound great. I think I'll stick with the kayaking, though. It was so cool being out there in the surf again."

"I have an idea," Katie said. "Nancy, why don't we take the whale-watching boat up there. You can drop Jenna, George, and me off for the kayaking, and then take the boat the rest of the way."

"That's a wonderful idea," Nancy agreed. "We'll probably be able to get a better view of everything—the pool and the property—from the boat."

While Ned paid the bill, the girls went into a small shop next door.

"I'm going to look for a kayak helmet," Jenna said. "I can't believe it, but I must have left mine at home."

"Can't you use the one you borrowed from Katie?" Bess asked.

"Not really," Jenna answered. "It's really important to me to use all my own stuff. It's hard to explain."

"I understand," George said. "Athletes don't like to borrow another athlete's gear. They want their own. They're almost superstitious about it."

"True," Jenna said. "After all," she added with a laugh, "I'm sure if I'd had my own helmet today, I'd have beat Katie big time."

"In your dreams," Katie said, poking her teammate with her elbow.

"Looks like you're out of luck," Bess said as she looked around the shop. "It's mostly jewelry and clothing."

"All handmade by local artisans," the shopkeeper said, joining them. "If you noticed the photographs on the wall as you came in, many celebrities have stopped here on their way along the coast and bought our things. Others have heard by word of mouth and placed custom orders. Please feel free to look around and let me know if I can help." She stepped away to greet another customer.

Nancy and the others wandered around the shop. As Nancy neared a display case of accessories, her heart skipped a beat. One particular item attracted her with its silvery gleam. It was a navy blue patent leather belt with a silver horse's head buckle. And it was exactly like the buckle that she had tugged from the rocky wall of the sea cave.

"Ah, you are drawn to one of my personal favorites, I see," the shopkeeper said as she swooped over. "There are only three of these in existence: the one you're admiring, this one"—she lifted her cardigan to show Nancy the one she herself was wearing—"and one that I sold recently."

The shopkeeper guided Nancy over to the wall of photographs. "Let me see, was that one bought by a celebrity? Hmmm . . . no, there it is. I don't recognize her as anybody, do you?"

The shopkeeper pointed to a photograph, and Nancy's heart skipped a beat again. The woman in the photo wearing the horse's head belt buckle was Joan Kim.

12

The List Lengthens

Nancy looked closely at the photo. "Did you say this woman bought the buckle recently?" she asked the shopkeeper.

"That's right. A couple of weeks ago, I believe."

"Was she just passing through the area, or does she live around here?" Nancy asked as Bess and George wandered over. She could tell by George's gasp that she had also noticed the photograph.

"She didn't say," the shopkeeper answered. "Would you like to see the buckle? I'll be happy to open the case for you."

"No, thank you," Nancy said.

"Well, let me know if you change your mind," the

shopkeeper said. She moved away to help Jenna with a sweater.

"Joan Kim," Bess said, under her breath.

"Wearing a buckle like the one Nancy found in the sea cave," George added.

"The buckle I found," Nancy said. "There were only three made, and two are here in the store."

"So, what's Joan Kim doing in a cave next to a whale holding pool?" George asked.

"Especially when she hates whale watching," Bess pointed out, her eyes wide.

"Exactly," Nancy said, adding, "I can't wait to get back out there tomorrow morning."

Ned joined them, and after they filled him in on the photograph, they all left for the drive back to Seabreak.

Back at the inn at last, Nancy, Bess, and Ned headed straight for their rooms and a welcome night's sleep.

The next morning Nancy couldn't wait to get started. She was still frustrated with her investigation for Katie and felt as if she'd run up against one dead end after another. She was eager to follow up on the discovery of the whale calf. What was it doing in a holding pool? And what did Joan Kim have to do with it—if anything?

After breakfast at Katie's, Nancy decided to call Sheriff Harvey. When she went to Katie's office,

Jenna was on the phone. "I can't believe you made me wait this long," she heard Jenna say. "I told you I was calling long-distance."

Then there was a pause while Jenna listened. Finally she spoke again. "Are you sure you didn't find my helmet? Well, call me at this number if it turns up." She put down the phone with a sigh and turned to Nancy. "I guess I'm in the market for a new helmet," she said, leaving the room.

Nancy called the sheriff. "I was trying to reach Katie," Sheriff Harvey said, "but her line was busy. I have Holt Scotto in my office right now. I'm going to question him about the bicycle accident and the stalking you reported in the cypress grove. Do you want to come down and make any further statements?"

"We'll be right there," Nancy said, hanging up the phone and grabbing Ned.

There was little traffic on the coast road, so Nancy and Ned arrived at the sheriff's office in record time. He gestured to them to take a seat at a long table. Holt Scotto sat on the other side of the table.

Sheriff Harvey began by asking Scotto his whereabouts on the night before last. Scotto hesitated while he seemed to think, and then said he was out on his boat.

The sheriff continued to question him, and then told him about being stalked in the cypress grove and about Bess's bicycle accident.

"I suppose they think I did it," Scotto said, flop-

106

ping his long arm out to point at Ned and Nancy. "Well, that's nuts!" he said fiercely. "I never did any of those things."

"Did you pile the rocks outside the door of that abandoned lighthouse down the coast?" Nancy asked. "And barricade my friend and me inside?"

Scotto looked up quickly, his eyes glaring at Nancy. He sputtered for a few minutes, then declared, "Yes! Yes, I did. And I'd do it again, just the same."

He turned to the sheriff. "I'd like to file a complaint," he said. "Against *her!*" He pointed at Nancy again. "She was trespassing," he continued. "Entering private property and walking around and all. Arrest her."

"Holt, what are you talking about?" Sheriff Harvey said. "You mean that lighthouse?"

"Yes, sir, I sure do," Scotto said. "It's for sale, and I'm thinking about buying it. I was down there looking at fishing sites, and I thought that old lighthouse might be a real buy. Then she came butting in and . . . and she tried to lock *me* in. That's what really happened. She tried to lock me in. She'd been following me all morning."

"That's exactly the opposite of what happened, Sheriff," Nancy said. "As I told you before, he followed us down the coast road. I thought he was going to ram my car."

"As I recall, he didn't follow you the entire time," Sheriff Harvey stated.

107

"No," Nancy said. "We turned off just in time and he drove on. Then when we came back to the lighthouse, his car was parked there—"

"So, he was actually at the lighthouse first," the sheriff said.

"See, I told you she was following me," Scotto said.

"Well, yes, he was," Nancy said. "But Bess wanted to see the lighthouse, and . . ." Nancy could see this was getting her nowhere and changed her line of attack. "Sheriff, if you'll recall, Mr. Scotto had already threatened me once at the inn. So, I was naturally on my guard."

"And you had warned him to stay away from Nancy and the rest of us," Ned pointed out.

"Then," Nancy continued, "we became concerned when someone appeared to be following us down the coast. He has now admitted that he was the driver and that he barricaded us in the lighthouse, which is further harassment. The night of the bicycle accident, his car was parked at the diner when we were there, but he wasn't inside. This would have given him opportunity to tamper with the bike in the parking lot."

"And the bike was definitely tampered with, right, Sheriff?" Ned said. "The axle was sawn partway through." Sheriff Harvey nodded.

"I wasn't at the diner that night," Scotto said. "I loaned my car to a friend 'cause I was out on my boat. How come we're letting outsiders cause so much trouble, Bradley?" he asked the sheriff. "I told everybody that Katie Firestone was going to cause trouble with her boat. See? It's happening."

"You'll have that friend that borrowed your car come down and make a statement, won't you," Sheriff Harvey said, ignoring Scotto's last statement. "I'd also like to talk to a few witnesses who can verify that you were fishing that evening."

"They'll be in today," Scotto promised.

"Speaking of the diner, Mr. Scotto," Nancy said, "I'm curious about something else."

"Yeah?" Scotto muttered, staring down at the table.

"Do you know Joan Kim? Where does she come from?" Nancy asked. "How did she end up in Seabreak that night? Did you invite her to talk to the fishermen?"

"Say, who's conducting this investigation, anyway?" Scotto asked, finally looking up.

"Just answer her questions, Holt," Sheriff Harvey said. He sounded fed up.

"I never met her before that night. She lives up north somewhere. She just showed up in town, saying she could help keep Seabreak free of whale watchers." His voice raised a pitch or two. "Seemed like a good idea to me," he yelled.

"All right, that's enough," the sheriff said. "Do you two have any more questions?" he asked Nancy and Ned. Nancy shook her head.

"All right, then," Sheriff Harvey said, "I'd like both you, Holt, and you, Ms. Drew, to stay away from each other. You are on opposite sides of a fence here. I want you to think of that fence as a real thing that separates you—and keeps you away from each other. Do you understand?"

He stood up and motioned Holt to leave, adding, "Holt, I want you to stay away from Katie, too, and all her friends and anyone else she brings to town. It's none of your business."

Scotto left the building, and the sheriff turned back to Nancy and Ned. Her cheeks flushed with irritation, Nancy nodded at him. "I know what you're going to say," she admitted. "You have no proof that Holt Scotto is the one causing all the trouble."

"That's right, Ms. Drew. I'll check out his alibi for the night before last, but—"

"But it'll probably be verified by his friends," Ned said. Nancy knew that Ned was disgusted and still suspected Scotto.

"That's right," the sheriff affirmed. "I need some kind of proof—even good circumstantial evidence. We've got next to nothing."

"Sheriff, while we're here," Nancy said, "I've got a couple of questions for you. What do you know about Andy Jason?"

"The whale-watching guy?" the sheriff answered. "I haven't heard anything negative. Why?"

Nancy told him about Jason's offers to Katie and how he seemed to have been hanging around a lot lately. "If Scotto does prove to be innocent, Jason's my second choice as suspect."

"Well, Jason's a real fireball of a businessman, I understand," Sheriff Harvey said. "But I haven't heard anything shady. I'll ask around."

"Good," Nancy said. "The second question is about a whale calf." Nancy and Ned told him about the previous day's adventure in the sea cave and about finding the holding pool.

"I can hardly believe it," Sheriff Harvey said. "It sounds strange to me. You might want to contact the Coast Guard. Marine problems are really their jurisdiction. I know what land you're talking about. It used to belong to the Purdy family, but I heard it was sold several months ago. Check with the county assessor's office next door. They might have some information for you."

He walked them to the door. "Now, stay away from Holt Scotto, Ms. Drew. He's definitely a hothead. But so far we've no proof he's broken the law."

Nancy and Ned thanked the sheriff, then checked in with the county assessor's office. The records there showed the property had been deeded to a corporation with the name of Shore Imports, Inc.

On the ride home, Nancy's thoughts were racing. "What if it's Joan Kim, Ned?" she asked.

"You mean causing all the problems?" Ned asked in return. "Do you think Joan Kim is the one trying to put Katie out of business?"

"She was in the diner to talk about ways to intimidate people who want to conduct whale-watching excursions," Nancy said. She was so excited by the possibility of solving this case, her words tumbled out. "No one invited her. She just showed up, Scotto said."

"If we can believe him," Ned grumbled.

"Look, every time we try to pin this thing on Scotto, we wind up down a blind alley. I'm not going to give him up entirely as a suspect, but I'm adding Joan Kim to our list. As far as I'm concerned, at this point, she and sneaky, always-seems-to-be-turning-up Andy Jason are right up there with Holt Scotto."

When they arrived at Katie's, everyone was waiting to hear what had happened. Over lunch Nancy and Ned filled them in quickly, winding up with Nancy's conclusions.

When they'd finished eating, Katie, George, and Jenna began gathering up their kayaking gear, and Ned helped them haul it down to the boat. Nancy told them she and Bess would be out in a minute. Then she went to the office to call the Coast Guard and suggested Bess check out Shore Imports, Inc., on the Internet.

The phone rang before either of them could get started. It was Sheriff Harvey, who reported that Holt Scotto's alibi for the night before last had been confirmed by nearly a dozen people.

Nancy called the Coast Guard and left a message

about the whale calf. Then Bess booted up the computer to search for Shore Imports, Inc.

It didn't take her long. The information was brief—only the address and contact information.

"Nancy, look!" Bess exclaimed.

As Nancy read the screen, her eyes opened wide at the name of the contact: Joan Kim, president.

13

Another Surprise

Nancy felt an electric current shoot through her. All the incidents that she and Katie had been a part of were tumbling around in her brain like jigsaw pieces poured from a box.

"Bess, this could be the breakthrough I've been looking for," she said.

"How, exactly?" Bess asked, printing out the data for Shore Imports, Inc.

"If Joan Kim is the one who has been harassing and threatening Katie . . . and if Joan Kim also owns the property near where we discovered the baby whale, then maybe the two situations overlap somehow."

"I guess so," Bess said. She looked a little confused. "But I don't see how, really. It seems to me you need more to put it all together."

"And we're going to get what we need today," Nancy said. "Let's get out to Katie's boat."

Nancy and Bess boarded the *Ripper* and headed up the coast to the area where they had been the day before.

Ned was familiar with Katie's boat, and he talked Katie into giving him the wheel. Nancy had piloted similar craft, so Ned gave her instructions on maneuvering this particular one through the sea.

On the way they passed a public fishing pier. "It's one o'clock," Katie said, looking at her watch. "We'll meet you three back here at the pier at five-thirty," Katie told Nancy.

Finally Katie found an area that she decided was perfect for their workout, and she, Jenna, and George launched their kayaks from the *Ripper*. Nancy piloted the boat for the next leg.

"Gee, everything looks so different from out here," Bess said, gazing at the shoreline.

"Partly because we're earlier and there's not much fog yet," Nancy said.

"It's a much clearer day," Ned agreed. "I didn't realize there were so many sea stacks around here. It looks like there are at least a couple big enough to be our sea cave. What if there's more than one cave? How will we know which one was the one we explored?"

"I'm not interested in the cave," Nancy said, turning the boat in toward shore a little. "I'm interested in that whale calf. And I suspect there's only one holding pool."

"I can't believe I'm actually going to see one up close," Bess said, hanging over the deck rail. "Are we close, do you think?"

"Ned, will you take the wheel?" Nancy asked. "I want to use the whale-watching telescope to find our way."

Ned took over the piloting, and Nancy and Bess sat down on the green- and white-striped banquette. It took Nancy a few minutes to adjust the lens, but at last she got a clear view of the seascape ahead and the landscape to their right.

"Well, we're leaving the populated area," she said, looking toward shore. I think we're close to the property of Shore Imports, Inc."

Bess took a turn looking through the scope. "I think I see a wire fence," she said.

Nancy swung the scope around to where Bess pointed. "That's it, Ned. The fence we climbed yesterday."

"I remember every step," Ned groaned. He skillfully turned the boat around the sea stacks. A couple of sea otters were sunbathing on the flat top of one rock about the size of the *Ripper*. Startled, they skidded down a well-worn path into the water.

As the boat chugged into the area of sea caves, the shoreline almost disappeared. From the ocean perspective, the rocky formations almost completely concealed the bluffs and landscape from anyone gliding by in a boat.

Nancy kept watching through the scope until she finally called out to the others. "There, I think I see it. Ned, let me have the wheel. I think I can get us right to it."

Nancy maneuvered the boat around two smaller sea caves until they finally faced an enormous rocky mound with a large opening.

"That's it, Nancy," Ned said. "I'm sure of it. That's our cave."

"Yep, and around behind it," Nancy said, turning the wheel, "should be—"

"The baby whale," Bess said almost in a whisper.

Nancy cut the motor to idle and rounded the sea cave, and there it was. The holding pen. The walls of the pen extended for yards and yards. She steered the boat carefully until they came up to the holding pen. It was perfectly situated among the huge rocks so that it was nearly invisible from shore or from farther out in the ocean.

"You know, we were lucky to find this thing," Ned said. "If we didn't know it was here, and were just out cruising, we'd have passed right by it."

"Listen, Ned," Nancy said, straining to hear.

"I don't hear anything," Ned said.

"I don't either," Bess said.

"That's what I mean," Nancy said, disappointed. "No whispers, no moans."

"No whale, I'll bet," Ned said, craning over the railing to see into the holding pool.

Nancy idled the boat around the oceanside perimeter of the pool. She remembered the treacherous rocks she had kayaked through yesterday to get back to shore. She knew better than to try to take the *Ripper* through them.

"Maybe it's just swimming under water," Bess said hopefully. Then she added, "I know, I know, they have to come up to the surface to breathe."

Nancy realized she was holding her breath, hoping the whale calf would surface. With a sigh, she realized that the pool was probably empty.

"I don't believe it," Bess said. "It's gone. You guys really did see it, didn't you?"

"Yes, we saw it," Ned said, looking into the pool through the telescope. His tone of voice indicated he was disappointed.

When they reached the far end of the holding pool, Nancy had to turn back out into the ocean to avoid running into a huge sea stack. The shoreline, with the backdrop of an enormous bluff, curved dramatically out into the water. The metal fence of Shore Imports, Inc., continued along the bluff top.

Nancy idled the boat on around the long curve of

land. On the far side of the curve, hidden by the bluff, was a harbor.

"Look at that!" Bess said, pointing into the harbor. "What is it?"

Nancy was stunned to see a huge ship apparently anchored about five hundred yards out in the harbor. "It looks like some sort of freighter," she suggested.

Cranes and pulleys jutted high into the air from the ship, forming sharp geometric shapes against the fog bank far on the horizon.

Nancy looked at the ship, then back at the shore. Because of the rocks in the sea and the enormous bluff, the ship was probably not visible from any road except one on the private property.

"I'll bet this is a private harbor for Joan Kim's outfit," Nancy guessed. "I think we need to check out that ship." She increased the speed of the boat and turned it toward the ship. "If anyone stops us, we're just tourists out for some sight-seeing. We're just interested in the pretty big ship and wondering what it is."

She steered the *Ripper* around the curve of land and into the harbor.

"One of you might want to aim the telescope toward the ship," she suggested, keeping her eye on the boat ahead. "See if you can tell how many people are wandering around on deck. Hey, is anybody listening to me back there? I don't think we'll get on board, but I'd like to know who owns it and—"

She felt a searing pain on the back of her head. Her knees felt like melted gelatin and the blood all seemed to rush from her head. The last thing she heard as she crumpled to the floor was a plaintive, unearthly moan.

14

Curious Cargo

The pain in the back of Nancy's head cascaded in waves. It would be just horrible for a few seconds, and then it would get worse.

As she regained consciousness, she felt as if her head were full of ocean fog. As wisps would clear away, bits of the world became clearer.

She tried to move her hands, but realized they were tied behind her—her ankles were tied as well. That gave her a jolt of awareness that seemed to clear masses of fog out of her brain. Her eyes opened partway.

She heard a rustling next to her and a groan. Opening her eyes wide, she looked toward the sound. The room was dark, but she still could recognize Bess's blond hair.

"Bess," Nancy whispered. "Bess, can you hear me?"

"Mmmhmmm," Bess mumbled. "My wrist—my wrist hurts."

Nancy raised up on one elbow. Just a thin strip of light shone from under a door. Nancy saw that Bess's wrists and ankles were also tied. She had an old red bandanna tied around her neck. "It's your sprained wrist, Bess," Nancy said. "Sit up. Let me see if I can loosen the rope."

Nancy sat up and scooted toward Bess so they were back to back. Then, blindly feeling the bindings around Bess's wrists, Nancy's fingers began picking at the ropes.

"It was two men," Bess said in a hushed voice. "They just appeared over the railing of the deck."

"They must have approached in a raft or rubber boat," Nancy said. "I never heard a thing."

"Neither did I or Ned," Bess whispered. "They just overpowered us. Ned put up quite a fight, but they hit him with a wrench. I tried to call out, but one of them had his hand over my mouth."

"Did they knock you out, too?" Nancy asked as she tugged and poked at Bess's wrist ropes.

"No. They tied this smelly old bandanna around my mouth as a gag. I kept rubbing my chin against my shoulder and managed to work the gag off. I've been trying to wake you up ever since."

"Ohhhhhh," groaned Ned from the corner of the small room. "Ooohhhhh."

"Shhh," Bess and Nancy both hushed Ned as he began to wake up.

"Where are we?" Ned mumbled. "What happened?"

"I have a feeling we're on the freighter," Nancy said. "Someone was not happy about our being so close."

"So, what do we do now?" Ned mumbled, following that with another groan.

"Are you okay, Ned?" Nancy asked.

"I'll live," Ned said. "But I want a piece of the guys who did this. Let's get out of here and find them."

Nancy could hear him thrashing around, probably trying to free himself from his bindings.

"Ned," Nancy said. "Scoot over here. Between the three of us, we ought to get free."

Nancy and Ned took turns working on Bess's wrist bindings. Finally, she was out of the ropes. With Bess's one good hand, and Ned's two tied ones pulling and twisting, Nancy's wrists were finally unbound.

They all kept working at the ropes, until at last they were all free. Nancy stood. Her legs were sore, but she could feel them getting stronger as she paced. "How's your head?" she asked Ned as he struggled to his feet. "Are you feeling dizzy?"

"A little," he answered. "But I'll be okay. I just need to move around a little. I think you're right about where we are. It sure feels like a ship—one that's anchored, not moving forward."

"How are you doing, Bess?" Nancy asked her friend. "How's your wrist?"

"I'm fine," Bess answered. "Let's get out of here. What kind of place is this? Where are we on the ship? It's so dark in here I can't see a thing."

"I know, but we don't dare turn on a light," Nancy said. They were all still talking in low tones, but no longer whispering. "Wherever we are, no one can hear us. If they could, they'd have been here by now. But I'm afraid to turn on a light. They might be able to see that somehow."

"Let's not leave these ropes," Nancy suggested. "They may come in handy—and the bandanna, too."

They each took the ropes that had bound their wrists and ankles and tied them around their waists. Each of Nancy's ropes wound around her twice.

"You can have this," Bess said, dangling the corner of the bandanna between her thumb and finger. "It smells like a gym sock."

Nancy stuffed the smelly bandanna in her back pocket, then stepped slowly around in the dark. She walked through taped-up cartons and wooden crates bound with thin strips of metal until she found a wall. Then she began feeling her way around it. She finally came to a light switch, but didn't push it up. Next to the switch was the metal door. "Locked, of course," she muttered under her breath. She was wary of speaking out loud near the door, in case someone could hear from the other side.

She continued her exploratory search around the perimeter of the room. So far, there appeared to be no other doors, no windows or portholes.

"I think we're in a hold belowdecks," she reported to the others, who had been doing their own tentative explorations. "Like a room where they keep the freight they're shipping."

"The *exports* of Shore Imports, Inc., right?" Ned added.

"Look for something we can use to get out of here—anything. Desk supplies, furniture, cleaning equipment."

"I found a table or a desk," Bess said. "Over here. It's stacked with boxes and completely surrounded with crates and cartons."

Nancy and Ned followed the sound of Bess's voice. They were standing near a wooden table. "Nothing," Ned said. "No drawer, no packing stuff, no scissors or paperclips. Nothing."

"Well, now there is something," Nancy said. "My foot has just bumped up against the perfect item." She reached under the table and rolled out a huge coil made up of one long strip of very thin, narrow metal that had been wound up into a wheel.

"What is it?" Bess asked, leaning down to get a better look.

"It's metal strapping," Ned said. "The stuff they

wind around cartons to keep them secure. Like rope, only stronger."

"And it's just what we need," Nancy said. The wheel was way too heavy to carry, so she just rolled it across the room to the door. Then she found the end of the coil. It was a flat piece of metal about a quarter inch wide, and it was perfect for picking a lock.

It took Nancy less than a minute to unlock the door. Before she opened it, she looked at her friends. She knew that if they were on the freighter, they were in great danger. They could be held prisoner indefinitely. They could even be taken to another location or another country.

"Our first goal is to get off this boat," she said. "We need to find a raft, a lifeboat, a motor launch—anything that we can use to get to shore. I don't know how long we were knocked out, but it's got to be at least four o'clock—maybe later. That means the fog is close or already in. So a getaway in another craft is a real option, because the fog will give us cover."

"What if someone sees us?" Bess asked.

"Or if we get separated?" Ned added.

"Our second goal is to contact the authorities. If we get separated, we each need to keep trying to find a way off the boat. Whoever makes it, needs to call the Coast Guard and get them out here immediately. I left a message for them before we left, so they may already be alerted. But we don't know that for sure."

Nancy's thoughts came quickly. "It's possible we

can even reach them from here," she continued. "Watch for phones, computers, anything we can use to communicate with the Coast Guard or someone on shore. Are you ready?"

"Okay, let's go," Ned said.

"The Three Musketeers," Bess said. Nancy could hear the wariness in her friend's voice. They gave one another high fives, and Nancy opened the door a tiny bit.

She peeked cautiously through the narrow opening. Then she opened it wider, then wider still.

There was no one in the long corridor. She led the others quietly down the hall.

They had only gone a few yards when a tremor of recognition rippled the hair on the back of Nancy's neck. From the end of the corridor came a familiar whisper and soft moan. They reached a set of double doors and cautiously pushed them open.

They were on a sort of balcony that extended out over the top of a large ten-foot-high hold that was apparently deep within the ship. At the bottom was a huge pool. Confined in a woven rope hammock submerged in the water was the baby whale.

"Oh, wow," Bess cried with a gasp. "Oh, I feel so sorry for it. They've got it sort of caught up. It looks like it can't swim or anything."

"But it looks safe," Ned said. "It can't injure itself and it's in the water."

"I don't care," Nancy said, as the whale stared up

at them and made that eerie sound. "It looks really sad—and sounds sad."

They watched the whale for another moment or two, then Nancy shook her head. "We can't stand here. We've got to get out. We're no help to ourselves or that calf as long as we're trapped on this boat. Let's try to get farther up in the ship."

They stepped cautiously back out into the corridor and ran down the hall. Skipping the elevator because it would make too much noise, they found a staircase and stepped quietly up to the next floor. A quick search of the corridor turned up nothing but locked doors. So they climbed to the next level.

From the stairwell, Nancy cracked the door to the corridor the tiniest bit so she could barely see through the opening with one eye. She heard people talking and immediately recognized one of the voices coming from a room across the hall.

"It's Joan Kim," Bess whispered behind Nancy. "I recognize her voice from when she spoke at the diner."

Nancy nodded, keeping the door open a paper-thin crack. A window across the hall revealed a sort of meeting or conference room. Two men and a woman were listening to Joan Kim.

"We'll take our usual route," she said. "We need to get the cargo to the client as soon as possible. We'll leave shortly, when the fog is densest."

"What about the prisoners?" the other woman asked.

"We will keep them comfortable and alive, as we do our cargo," Joan Kim answered. "When we reach our destination, we will turn them loose and they can fend for themselves."

"But it's a dangerous country," the other woman pointed out. "They may be shot just for being there. Or imprisoned."

"They will no longer be our responsibility at that point," Kim responded. Then she dismissed the others and sat down at a desk in the corner of the room. Nancy could see by the large portholes on the outer wall of the room that they were on an upper deck.

The other woman and the two men started toward the door of the meeting room, and Nancy eased her stairway door closed. She and Ned held the door shut with all their strength, in case any of the people intended to use that door. But Nancy heard the footsteps of the three get fainter and fainter as they apparently walked the opposite way down the corridor.

Nancy knew they didn't dare go out into that corridor as long as Joan Kim was in the meeting room. So she led Bess and Ned up the staircase to the next landing. A quick check of that corridor showed it to be empty. Nancy stepped out first and started down the hall.

Suddenly she heard a man's voice speaking from right around the corner ahead of her—and he was coming her way. Thinking fast, she tried the first door she came to. It was unlocked. She ducked inside and locked the door behind her. She stood very still in the dark room, barely breathing. Stay in the stairwell, Bess and Ned, she thought, trying to will her friends out of trouble. Don't come into the hallway.

She heard at least two sets of footsteps pass by the door. "I don't like taking along extra cargo, if you know what I mean," the man said as they passed. "I say we get rid of them now."

She heard someone unlock another door and open it. Then she heard the footsteps again, the door closed, and it was quiet. Where are Bess and Ned? she wondered. Are they still in the stairwell? Did they come out, hear the voice, and duck into another room the way I did?

Nancy thought for a moment about what she should do, then decided to make a run for it to try to find her friends, a boat, or a way to call for help. As she reached for the door, she heard the lock turn.

Nancy backed into the small room, looking for an escape route, but she could see none.

She watched in dismay as the doorknob turned and the door creaked open. The light suddenly shot on, and standing in the doorway was Joan Kim.

15

The Scrap of Evidence

The harsh bright light made Nancy blink. Adrenaline seemed to electrify her as she stood face-to-face with Joan Kim.

"Ms. Drew," the tall, attractive woman said. She was dressed in a purple silk jumpsuit and held one hand behind her back. Frowning, she stepped inside the door and shut it behind her.

Nancy looked around quickly. They were in a small dining room, perhaps an area used for entertaining clients or guests. There were three round tables set with white linen cloths and napkins. In the middle of each table were two silver candlesticks and a silver salt and pepper shaker.

"I had heard you were very skillful," Joan Kim

continued. "It appears my sources were correct. You have managed to thwart my crew's best efforts to keep your activities restricted."

"How do you know who I am?" Nancy asked. She knew she needed to stall the woman until she could figure out what to do.

Behind Kim's shoulder, Nancy saw a window into the hall. The light was so bright in the room, she could barely see through the window. Instead, she saw a reflection of the room itself.

"I have amassed quite a file on Ms. Firestone. I know who her friends are and who her enemies are. I have had people try to frighten her into going out of business. I have followed her myself on occasion. I even followed you one evening." Kim's lips stretched into a slim smile.

"On the bluffs, in the cypress grove."

"That's correct," Joan Kim said with an eager nod. "I was in town anyway, preparing for my speech in the diner. When I saw you all file by on your bicycles, I assumed Ms. Firestone was with you, so I followed you out to the bluffs."

As Joan Kim talked, Nancy inched to her right. Kim instinctively moved also, until she stood partly in front of the window. In the reflection, Nancy got the information she was seeking. Kim held a gun behind her back. Now Nancy knew her only hope was to surprise and incapacitate her at the same time.

"When I discovered Ms. Firestone was not one of

the bikers," Joan Kim continued, "I changed my plans slightly and chose you as my target. I thought it might give you something to think about.

"I checked with some of my resources about you," she continued. "You have quite a reputation in some places for being a detective. You have proved that today, for here you are."

"Do you know what the sentence is for kidnapping, Ms. Kim?" Nancy asked.

"It is of no interest to me, because we will not be here much longer. When we arrive at our destination, you will be released, so there will be no more kidnapping."

"Where are we going exactly?" Nancy asked.

"Across the Pacific," Kim said in a clipped voice. "I have business there."

"Does this business have anything to do with that whale calf in the pool below?" Nancy asked. She could hardly keep the anger out of her voice when she thought of the captive creature.

"So you took a tour," Kim said. Her eyes flashed at Nancy. "Very well, I'll share my plans with you. You can do nothing about them. I have a large—and lucrative—business. I own ships around the world and capture whale calves to sell to our clients."

"Isn't it illegal to capture a migrating calf?" Nancy asked. She was standing near one of the tables. She shuffled her feet, each shuffle moving her back an inch or two until she felt the edge of the table against her hip. She reached back to lean on the table. "What do your clients do with them?" Nancy asked, not sure she wanted to hear the answer.

"It's not my concern," Kim said, with an offhand gesture. "Some are put in zoos or films or other such attractions. Some are probably eaten."

As Joan Kim spoke, Nancy reached back until her fingers closed around one of the salt or pepper shakers. Easing it toward her, she simultaneously began twisting off the top. The lid fell silently onto the tablecloth. Nancy dipped her finger into the shaker. Her heart leapt with an elated rush when she felt the contents—it had a powdery, not a grainy, feel. Good, I got the pepper, she thought. She picked up the open pepper shaker and held it carefully up and under the back of her sweater.

"This is why I am determined to keep whale-watching businesses and the tourists they attract out of my way," Kim continued.

"So you *are* the one responsible for all the trouble Katie has been having," Nancy said, pouncing on her opening.

Joan Kim looked at Nancy. She didn't seem to notice that Nancy had moved back a foot or two. "But she wasn't discouraged," Kim said. "And you weren't either. You just kept coming. I should have been far more aggressive out on those bluffs. Then I wouldn't have to deal with you and your friends right now. Where are the other two, by the way?"

"And you—or someone working for you—sawed the axle on Bess's bike, too, right?" Nancy said quickly, trying to keep the woman distracted and talking. "And vandalized Katie's boat?"

The woman seemed taken aback by Nancy's words. "Bicycle axle?" she repeated. "I know nothing about that. And I did nothing to Ms. Firestone's boat. I considered it, but someone beat me to it."

She took a couple of steps toward Nancy, then stopped. "No more questions from you," she said. "Only answers. Where are your friends?"

"Did you know I found your horse's head buckle?" Nancy asked abruptly, hoping to get her captor off guard.

Joan Kim's expression softened immediately. "My buckle? Where did you find it? It's one of my favorite pieces. Give it back to me now!"

"I found it in the sea cave next to the offshore holding pool," Nancy said.

"Ah yes," Kim said, with a smile. "I sometimes go there for solitude and peace. A few weeks ago I took an unexpected spill from my canoe. Where is my buckle?" Her eyes were open wide with anticipation.

Keeping the pepper shaker under her sweater, Nancy pulled her hand around to the front. With both hands under her sweater, she pretended to be unbuckling a belt. Then with one quick, sure gesture, she pulled the shaker out from under her sweater, and, leaning forward, dashed the contents in Joan Kim's face. Then Nancy reached back immediately and grabbed a candlestick from the table.

"What! What have you done!" Her left arm came out from behind her back, but her eyes were clenched tightly against the pepper. Nancy was ready for her, slamming the candlestick into the woman's arm with a solid blow.

The gun flew across the room, landing in a soft easy chair in the far corner. Joan Kim doubled over. Her left arm hung limp. Her right hand swiped frantically at the pepper dust on her face.

As Nancy grabbed her arms, the woman tried to fight, but she was stunned by the pepper. Tears rippled out from her eyelids and rolled in streaky patterns down the black-and-gray speckles covering her cheeks. Her nose ran, and she tried to yell for help. But with every breath, she inhaled more pepper. The only sounds that came out were gagged squeaks and coughing spasms.

Within minutes, Nancy had tied Joan Kim to a heavy radiator against the wall. She tied the bandanna around her mouth as a gag. She didn't pull it too tight, because the woman was still having trouble breathing.

Just being around Joan Kim made Nancy's eyes sting, so she held her breath as long as she could and moved quickly. She took the keys from Kim's pocket and then checked the room for a phone. There was none. She slipped the ammunition cartridge out of the gun and into her pocket, left the room, and locked the door.

Out in the corridor, Nancy took a few deep breaths and listened for anyone who might be nearby. Hearing nothing, she made her way down the hallway to a door leading to the open deck.

She looked through the glass door and saw Ned and Bess at the far end of the deck. They were standing very still, not talking. In front of them, his back to Nancy, was a man. She could tell by their postures that the man was probably armed.

Nancy looked around the deck for something she could use to help her friends. Her eyes stopped on a large metal basket by the railing. "Yes!" she said under her breath. "That's it!"

She opened the door very slowly. Bess and Ned saw her, but they immediately focused back on the man without giving her away. Nancy heard Ned start a conversation to distract the man.

Nancy stepped onto the deck and closed the door silently behind her. She inched over to the metal basket. Inside was an emergency flare gun and cartridges, like the ones Katie had given her. She picked up the large flare gun and opened the muzzle. She placed the cartridge inside, pointed the flare gun up and fired it in the air.

With a whistling surge, the flare arched through the fog and exploded its fireworks.

When the flare's whistle began, Nancy ducked

behind a stack of coiled ropes. The man at the end of the deck whirled around, but Ned butted his head into the man's back and knocked him to the ground. While Nancy set off another flare, Ned knocked the man out with one perfect punch and tied him up.

Through the fog, Nancy heard the continuous honking siren of the Coast Guard. Soon she saw the boat coming toward the ship.

"Are you two okay?" Nancy asked.

"Yeah," Bess answered, "but we were worried about you."

"I'm fine," Nancy said. "And you'll be happy to hear that Joan Kim is wearing the smelly bandanna."

"Whoa," Ned said. "You ran into her?"

"You could say that," Nancy replied with a smile. "I'll tell you about it later. It looks as if we're about to be rescued."

Nancy pointed to the welcome sight of the Coast Guard boat plowing through the fog. Through a speaker, the CG officer ordered the ship's crew to surrender. The few that were still aboard appeared on deck with their hands over their heads.

Nancy, Ned, and Bess told their stories to one of the CG officers who boarded the ship.

"We received your phone message, Ms. Drew," the officer said, "so we were already in the area, checking out the offshore holding pool. We were heading out to inspect the ship when we saw your flare. We would have been here sooner, but we had to stop to pick up the motor launch carrying some of Joan Kim's colleagues, who were trying to escape."

The door opened on to the deck, and two other officers brought out Joan Kim and took her to the ladder leading down to the Coast Guard boat.

"Kim has a legitimate importing business that we were aware of," the officer told Nancy. "But we sure didn't know anything about her illegal sideline. You and your friends are true heroes."

"What will happen to the baby whale?" Bess asked.

"We'll turn it over to some people who are specialists in whale behavior. They'll determine what's best for the calf. If it's healthy, it may be released now. Or it may be held until the adult whales return and be released then."

The Coast Guard had picked up Katie's boat and towed it to the ship. When the CG finished questioning them, Nancy and her friends finally headed south toward the fishing pier where Katie, George, and Jenna waited.

Ned docked the *Ripper*, and they all went into a seafood restaurant on the pier for dinner. Nancy, Ned, and Bess regaled the other three with their experiences aboard Joan Kim's boat.

"Nancy, I can't thank you enough for solving the case," Katie said. "I can finally do my cruises and not worry about harassment—or worse."

"I appreciate your thanks," Nancy said, "but I'm not convinced the case is totally solved."

"What do you mean?" Jenna asked.

"Well, we still don't know who trashed the *Ripper* and who tampered with the bike," Nancy pointed out.

"It wasn't Joan Kim?" George asked.

"She really didn't seem to know anything about either one," Nancy said.

"Then it must be Holt Scotto," Jenna concluded.

"Both Kim and Scotto confessed to causing some of the trouble," Nancy said. "There would be no reason for them to hold back on those other two things."

"I still don't like Andy Jason," George said. "What about him?"

"I haven't ruled him out," Nancy said, "but he doesn't really seem to be trying to run Katie out of business. He seems to want to work *with* her. It doesn't make sense that he'd try to hurt her, like with the bike accident."

After dinner they all boarded the *Ripper* for the cruise back to Katie's.

"So, you heard all about our day," Nancy said to George, joining her on the banquette. "How was yours? How did the workout go?"

"Pretty well, actually," George said. "Katie and Jenna treat it like a war, though. Kind of takes some of the fun out of it."

"They're fierce competitors," Nancy observed. "That's what makes them champions."

"Yeah, and Katie told me some stuff that explains why they go at each other so hard," George said, lowering her voice. "They've got kind of a history together. Jenna was a regular world team member until Katie came along. Katie was so good that she was moved into Jenna's place on the team and Jenna became an alternate."

"So Jenna's trying to get back on the team, and Katie's trying to hold on to her place," Nancy concluded. "No wonder their workouts are so tough. I'm amazed they even speak to each other."

"Katie says the team comes first," George said. "That's why she invited Jenna down. It will help them get along better and keep the peace."

When they got back to land, they made their usual date for breakfast at Katie's and then hit their beds.

Bess fell asleep immediately, but Nancy's thoughts kept her awake. She was happy about solving the mystery of the baby whale, but she still had work to do. *I promised I'd help Katie,* she told herself, *and I'm going to.* After hours of tossing and turning, she finally fell asleep.

Nancy awoke the next morning with a jolt. Her mind was racing. She remembered the beginning of the note that was waiting for her when she and Bess got home the night of Bess's accident: *So sorry your friend got hurt* . . . "There is only one person who could have known about Bess's injury and been able to get a note under this door before we got home," she mumbled. "I've got to talk to Katie."

She pulled on jeans and a lightweight yellow sweater. Then she wrote a note for Bess telling her where she was going.

She ran the mile to Katie's house, but when she got there, no one was home. George runs in the morning. They're probably all out on the bluff. She let herself in with the key Katie had lent her.

She ran straight to Katie's office and rummaged through the drawers until she found a phone book. Then she dialed the phone company customer service representative.

"Hello, this is Katie Firestone," she said. "I forgot to record a long-distance call I made yesterday. Could you please give me the number?"

She wrote the number down and dialed it immediately. It rang twice, then someone answered. "Good morning," the voice said. "Malone Motel."

16

Blowup on the Bluff

"Is anyone there?" said the voice on the other end of the phone. "This is the Malone Motel."

In her mind's eye, Nancy saw the scrap of business card she found on Katie's vandalized boat. *Malone Motel* fit perfectly.

"Uh, yes," Nancy said, thinking fast. "This is Jenna Deblin. I was there earlier this week."

"Yes, Ms. Deblin," the voice said. "I talked to you yesterday about your stay with us on Sunday night. You were asking about a sea kayak helmet, I believe."

"That's correct," Nancy said. She was so excited, she had to concentrate on making her voice calm.

"We tried to call you," the voice said. "We did find

your helmet after all. Would you like us to send it to you—or just hold it for your return visit with us."

"Hold on to it," Nancy said. "About how many miles are you from Seabreak?" she asked.

"Let me see," the voice said. "Why, I'd say two hundred miles at the most."

"Thank you," Nancy said. As Nancy was hanging up the phone, George burst through the door.

"Hey, you're early," George said, panting from her run. "Where are Bess and Ned?" She looked at Nancy. "What is it? You look like you've seen a ghost."

"Where are Katie and Jenna?" Nancy asked.

"They're probably on the bluff out by Katie's boat. There's a nice jogging trail out there."

"Come on, George," Nancy said, racing for the garage. "We've got to find them!"

Nancy and George grabbed a couple of bikes and headed out along the shore from Katie's house. After about twenty minutes, they finally saw two figures up ahead, jogging on the trail. Even from a distance, Nancy recognized immediately the tall, long-limbed form of Katie and the smaller lithe body of Jenna.

"There they are," George said, pointing ahead.

Nancy nodded and pedaled faster. As she watched, Katie and Jenna stopped jogging. Katie leaned over and stretched a little. Then she sank down into the golden grass and leaned back on her hands, looking up at the sky.

"Katie!" Nancy yelled as loud as she could against

the sea breeze, but Katie didn't seem to hear. "Jenna!" Nancy yelled again.

While Nancy and George watched, Jenna walked a little farther away, then leaned down and seemed to pick something up. Then she walked in from the bluff's edge a little, until she was out of Katie's line of vision.

Nancy could still see her, and she could also see the large cypress branch she held in her hand. Nancy pedaled faster and faster. Her heart was in her throat and she felt as if her lungs would burst.

"Katie!" Nancy yelled again. Then George seemed to realize what was happening and yelled for her friend, too. Katie seemed to be totally oblivious. She looked as if she were deep in thought as she rested on the bluff.

In horror, Nancy watched as Jenna crept behind Katie and lifted the large hunk of gray cypress high over Katie's head.

"Katie!" Nancy screamed with all her strength, and this time it worked. Katie sat straighter and looked around. She saw Jenna just in time to duck.

When Jenna saw Nancy and George approaching, she looked frantically around and then began running away. The trail was her only escape, but it was hopeless.

Nancy and George whizzed right by Katie and caught up with Jenna, who slowed to a walk and stopped. Then she dropped to her knees in a dejected heap on the trail and gave in to desperate, draining sobs.

Nancy and George got off their bikes as Katie ran up to join them.

"Jenna!" Katie said. "What were you doing? What on earth were you thinking?"

"She wasn't thinking about anything but herself," Nancy explained. "And her past glory on the sea kayak team."

"She's been jealous of you for a long time," George added. "You knew that, Katie."

"Yes, but I didn't think she'd go this far," Katie said. She looked a little dazed.

"When did you really get to Seabreak, Jenna?" Nancy asked. "By the way, I talked to the Malone Motel this morning. I already know the answer."

Jenna looked as if she was going to try to run away again, but finally, her shoulders dropped. Between spurts of anger and hysterical sobs, she spoke. "Monday," she confessed. "I got into the area on Monday."

"But you didn't come to my place until Tuesday," Katie said. "I don't get it. Where were you?"

"I slept in my car on a beach down the coast a couple of miles," Jenna said.

"But why?" Katie asked. She still seemed in shock.

"So she could wreck your boat," Nancy pointed out. "Right, Jenna?"

Jenna nodded. "I watched you," she told Katie. "You were so busy getting ready for Nancy and the others, you didn't even notice. In the middle of the night Monday, I went aboard the *Ripper.*"

"And ripped it," George said, in a disgusted voice.

"Same question," Katie said, her voice low and sad. "Why? Why would you want to ruin my business?"

"It's only fair," Jenna lashed out. "You ruined me. You took away the only thing I ever wanted—a regular spot on the national team. I don't care about your silly old whale watching. But I figured if I disabled your boat, maybe you'd be too distracted to compete. Or, better yet, maybe you'd have an accident."

Nancy got a chill when she saw the nasty look on Jenna's face.

"How did you figure it out, Nancy?" Katie asked. "How did you know it was Jenna?"

"I realized that Jenna was the only person who could have put the note under my door the night Bess fell off the bike, because she was the only one besides us who knew about the accident that quickly. She found out about it when we called you, Katie."

"That's right," Katie said. "I told her right away."

"So while we were down at the clinic, she was slipping the note under the door," George concluded.

"You're also the one who cut the axle, aren't you?" Nancy asked Jenna.

"Yes," Jenna hissed. "But it was Katie's bike. *She* was supposed to have the accident."

Katie, George, and Nancy walked Jenna back to

Katie's house. Ned and Bess were there. While George and Katie filled them in, Nancy called the sheriff. They all held Jenna until Sheriff Harvey picked her up.

That evening Nancy, Katie, George, Bess, and Ned fixed a celebration dinner of grilled tuna and homemade fries.

"I've decided that if Jenna will agree to get counseling, I won't press charges," Katie said. "She needs serious help here, not prison. Besides, when the world kayaking organization hears about this, she'll be banned for life."

"That will punish her more than anything," Bess said sadly.

Ned laughed out loud as he helped himself to a third helping of fries.

"What's so funny?" Bess asked.

"I was just thinking about the first time we talked about taking this trip. I knew I'd like the kayaking, but I figured the rest of the time would be a big snooze. Was I ever wrong."

"You should have known better, Ned," George reminded him. "We all know that when we go on vacation with Nancy Drew, we're guaranteed a whale of a good time!"

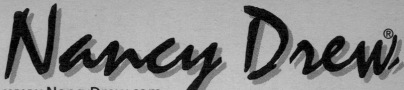

**Do your younger brothers and sisters
want to read books like yours?**

**Let them know there
are books just for *them!***

They can join Nancy Drew and her best
friends as they collect clues and solve
mysteries in

THE

NANCY DREW

NOTEBOOKS®

Starting with
#1 The Slumber Party Secret
#2 The Lost Locket
#3 The Secret Santa
#4 Bad Day for Ballet

AND

**Meet up with suspense and mystery
in The Hardy Boys® are: The Clues Brothers™**

Starting with
#1 The Gross Ghost Mystery
#2 The Karate Clue
#3 First Day, Worst Day
#4 Jump Shot Detectives

A MINSTREL® BOOK
Published by Pocket Books

2324

The Fascinating Story of One of the World's Most Celebrated Naturalists

Celebrating 40 years with the wild chimpanzees

MY LIFE with the CHIMPANZEES

by JANE GOODALL

From the time she was girl, Jane Goodall dreamed of a life spent working with animals. Finally, when she was twenty-six years old, she ventured into the forests of Africa to observe chimpanzees in the wild. On her expeditions she braved the dangers of the jungle and survived encounters with leopards and lions in the African bush. And she got to know an amazing group of wild chimpanzees—intelligent animals whose lives bear a surprising resemblance to our own.

Illustrated with photographs

A Byron Preiss Visual Publications, Inc. Book

A Minstrel® Book
Published by Pocket Books

2403